JOHN BLACKBURN

The Winds of Midnight

VALANCOURT BOOKS

The Winds of Midnight by John Blackburn
Originally published in Great Britain by Jonathan Cape in 1964
First U.S. edition published by Mill & Morrow in 1964 under the title
Murder at Midnight
First Valancourt Books edition 2024

Published by Valancourt Books, Richmond, Virginia
http://www.valancourtbooks.com

ISBN 978-1-960241-30-6 (*trade paperback*)
Also available as an electronic book.

Set in Dante MT
Cover by Pedro Marques

THE WINDS OF MIDNIGHT

JOHN BLACKBURN was born in 1923 in the village of Corbridge, England, the second son of a clergyman. Blackburn attended Haileybury College near London beginning in 1937, but his education was interrupted by the onset of World War II; the shadow of the war, and that of Nazi Germany, would later play a role in many of his works. He served as a radio officer during the war in the Mercantile Marine from 1942 to 1945, and resumed his education afterwards at Durham University, earning his bachelor's degree in 1949. Blackburn taught for several years after that, first in London and then in Berlin, and married Joan Mary Clift in 1950. Returning to London in 1952, he took over the management of Red Lion Books.

It was there that Blackburn began writing, and the immediate success in 1958 of his first novel, *A Scent of New-Mown Hay*, led him to take up a career as a writer full time. He and his wife also maintained an antiquarian bookstore, a secondary career that would inform some of Blackburn's work, including the bibliomystery *Blue Octavo* (1963). *A Scent of New-Mown Hay* typified the approach that would come to characterize Blackburn's twenty-eight novels, which defied easy categorization in their unique and compelling mixture of the genres of science fiction, horror, mystery, and thriller. Many of Blackburn's best novels came in the late 1960s and early 1970s, with a string of successes that included the classics *A Ring of Roses* (1965), *Children of the Night* (1966), *Nothing but the Night* (1968; adapted for a 1973 film starring Christopher Lee and Peter Cushing), *Devil Daddy* (1972) and *Our Lady of Pain* (1974). Somewhat unusually for a popular horror writer, Blackburn's novels were not only successful with the reading public but also won widespread critical acclaim: the *Times Literary Supplement* declared him 'today's master of horror' and compared him with the Grimm Brothers, while the *Penguin Encyclopedia of Horror and the Supernatural* regarded him as 'certainly the best British novelist in his field' and the *St James Guide to Crime & Mystery Writers* called him 'one of England's best practicing novelists in the tradition of the thriller novel'.

By the time Blackburn published his final novel in 1985, much of his work was already out of print, an inexplicable neglect that continued until Valancourt began republishing his novels in 2013. John Blackburn died in 1993.

By John Blackburn

* Available from Valancourt Books

I

He drove home through the dull morning light and he was drunk—very drunk indeed, but not entirely because of alcohol, though he'd had a skinful. The Bull at Raynford: a small whisky. The George and Dragon at Selwicke: a double. The place farther south with a name he couldn't remember, though there had been cards advertising it laid out along the bar counter: two more doubles and several pints of warm, gassy bitter beer. There was also the flask in his pocket which must lie almost three-quarters empty by now.

Yes, as they said, he'd had a skinful all right, but why the hell shouldn't he? Hadn't he a reason for it? The best reason in the world, or one of the best. He grinned foolishly for a moment, and then his eyes fell on the speedometer and he braked hard. Seventy-five! That was crazy. Seventy-five miles an hour down the wet suburban streets, with the "40" restriction signs flashing past like telegraph poles seen from a train and the roar of his cracked exhaust an invitation to every lurking police car. "Here I am, boys, come and get me."

But just where had he broken that damned exhaust pipe? Up in the Lake District, was it, when he'd tried to drive across the moor and skidded against a boulder? Two days ago—three? No, he couldn't even remember that. All he could remember was what had happened at a place called Sedale. The knowledge that had come to him just before he started to write the final chapter of his book. The complete and utter realization that part of his life was finished, washed-up, done for.

Only forty miles an hour now, that was better. Though he might be finished he had to know the rest of the story and he didn't want to go out that way. A wheel spinning slowly on its side, blood and oil dribbling on to the tarmac and a narrow

column in the centre pages of the *Thames Valley Gazette*—
"Tragic Death of Local Author—The deceased, who had con-
sumed the equivalent of twelve small whiskies and was also
suffering from the effects of carbon monoxide poisoning . . ."

But he hadn't far to go. He wound down the window a little
more, feeling a spatter of thin rain on his forehead and smelling damp grass and lime trees as he crossed Ealing Common.
Yes, only a little way. Just three miles to the place where he
might learn the truth. On the Great West Road the factory
signs still blazed out, though there was only himself and a
few indifferent lorry drivers to see them, and already the sky
was growing lighter. He slowed at the roundabout, hearing
his exhaust note hammer against the pillars of the flyover,
and turned south; the sour smell of the river replacing grass
and diesel fumes and the church on Kew Green looking like a
Gothic ruin in the drizzle.

Just a mile and a half now. The gate of the Botanical Gardens slid past him, an electric train rattled in the distance, the
long, tree-lined street seemed to stretch endlessly in front
of him, but at last he turned into a cul de sac and switched
off the engine. As always, the low block of flats looked quiet
and peaceful and ultra-respectable. Apart from a light in the
entrance, every window was dark and all the tenants would
still be asleep. All except one tenant, that was. His hands flexed
against the steering wheel for a second and then he climbed
heavily out, leaving his bag on the seat behind him. He
wouldn't be sleeping at home any more. What he had to do
would only take a few minutes.

But they'd been happy there once! Their first real home
after two years of furnished digs. The familiar secure smell
of the place wrapped around him as he climbed up the stairs:
pinewood and lavender polish mingling with the dryness of
radiators. He'd paid the deposit for the flat with the American
book club advance on his second novel. What was the title
again? *Cinderella in Carthage*. A damn silly title for a damn poor
book, but somehow it had caught on and he'd rushed round

to the estate agents on the morning he'd received the cheque.

And here he was—home! The cream-painted door with the Y-shaped scar on the panel which he'd meant to touch up a score of times but somehow never got round to; the dolphin knocker, the bell push, the brass plaque reading "Mr. & Mrs. Wm. Irwin."

Yes, Mr. and Mrs. Irwin. That was just a joke now, it seemed. Bill Irwin, aged thirty-two, author of eight untalented, pot-boiling romantic novels churned out without love to obtain a middle-class standard of living and Mrs. Irwin. Mrs. Mary Irwin whom he'd never really known after five years of what he thought was a happy marriage. Mary Irwin—bitch!

He fiddled drunkenly with his key, missing the lock by inches at first, and then slid it home. "A key to the door"—"a roof over one's head"—"an Englishman's home is his castle." The phrases ran through his head as he stepped into the hall. Though it was in darkness, he knew every inch of the place by heart and didn't bother to turn on the lights. On the right, the sitting room, the dining room, the kitchen. To the left, his room: study, office, den or cage, whichever way you chose to look at it. Beyond that, their—her bedroom.

But he didn't go into the bedroom at once. He stood in the open doorway, dreading what he knew he might find, listening to his watch ticking in time to his heart and at last reaching for the light switch and hearing a stranger's voice say, "Mary, Mary, my dear, I came back. I had to. You see I found the . . ."

And that was quite crazy, of course. She wasn't there. She couldn't be. She was miles away, if what he suspected was true. There was nothing in the flat except memories and furniture and clothes. The dressing table, the sofa, the tall looking glass, which she'd bought with her last bonus from the firm, the big blue bed . . .

Very cautiously, like a man who has just come out of prison after many years and fears the outside world, Bill Irwin examined his wife's room. There was no note for him and she hadn't left in a hurry, that was definite. In the wardrobe the dresses hung in ordered lines, the rows of bottles were neatly arranged on the dressing table and the nightgown on the pillow was folded for her return.

He knelt down beside the bed, feeling tears in his eyes as he stared at the nightgown and smelled a trace of her perfume. He felt completely alone and then suddenly knew that he was not alone at all. Just behind him something was moving.

"Mary," he said. "So you didn't go, darling. You didn't go, or you changed your mind and came home." Even as he spoke, he knew that it was impossible. She'd gone all right, and she wouldn't change her mind.

But there was something moving in the room. Something that seemed to be creeping very softly across the carpet towards him. The cat? No, that was just as impossible. The cat was miles away too; safe and snug in Winnie's Kittyhome, with a rubber mouse and two square meals a day in return for the thirty shillings a week which he could ill afford.

Not Mary—not the cat—not a mouse; no mouse could gnaw its way through the concrete and steel of Riverside Court. Something that had no right to be there.

With his heartbeats quickening, Bill turned towards the sound behind him. He saw the carpet, the rug in front of the dressing table, the legs of the sofa, the hem of the chintz curtains and the thing that looked quite out of place in the very feminine room. A boot—two old leather boots coming towards him, with the trousers above them spreading into a thick waist. He heard a sound of breathing, saw a gloved hand lift something black and start to bring it down. The floor tilted, spun round and threw him sideways into darkness.

In the beginning there was nothing except the darkness, though sometimes pictures drifted through it like grey photograph negatives. The pictures showed scenes of summer, with feet running across grass, and faces laughing in the grey sun, and hands clutching together. None of the pictures were real and soon the darkness swallowed them up again.

But on the second day there were lights, and they were real. Very dim lights at first, but they brightened with time to show more faces which didn't smile. These faces spoke to him, but he couldn't answer them and they seemed to be a long way away or viewed from the wrong end of a telescope. One face was dark and the other a pinkish white.

And on the fourth day he could make out what the voices were saying. The pink face had a Scots accent and the black face a thick drawl. Soon he even knew their names. "Come on, laddie. Wake up, my puir laddie," said Sister Lucy Angus of Fort William, Invernessshire. "Snap out of it, boy. Thar's mah boy," said Nurse Icylma Jackson of Spanish Town, Jamaica.

At last he even knew the owner of the hands. Two big, gingery hands that seemed to run over his head and pull back his eyelids at least twice a day, and the comforting, familiar smells that came with them: carbolic soap in the morning which was still there at night, but pleasantly mingled with the reek of brandy and cigar smoke.

There was also a rich, self-confident voice that went with those prying hands. "Poor devil," it said. "Must have taken quite a toss—dreadful shock after it as well—enough to unhinge a saint—thin skull too. Don't know if I ever told you, Sister, but I once had a similar experience myself. Fell off the spire of Saint Jerome's when I was a student—trying to place a certain utensil there—blacked out for forty-eight hours. Fortunately for me I've got a skull as thick as a ruddy ape's—not like this poor devil." The sound of knuckles tapping a forehead, fingers running across his eyes, and the whiff of cigar smoke creeping closer.

"Better, eh, old man? Be right as rain soon. Couple of weeks from now and you'll be having a good laugh about all this. Oh, sorry—terribly sorry. Bloody fool thing to have said under the circumstances, Sister. Hope he didn't hear me." The sound of heavy footsteps moving away and—darkness again.

But on the fifth day he opened his eyes fully and saw everything. The neatly tucked-in sheets at the end of the steel bed, the walls of the little white room, the black nurse standing by the window, and the huge gingery face beaming down at him.

"Well, old boy," said the face. "So you're finally out of it. Know where you are? Know who I am?"

"Yes, yes, of course." Bill struggled to concentrate. "This is the East Surrey County Hospital, and you are Dr. Harbinger; Dr. Raymond Harbinger. I think I owe you a great deal, Doctor."

"Ah, good! Very good, in fact! You've taken in quite a lot, it seems. Yes, Ray Harbinger at your service, but no thanks are necessary. I get paid for what I do." A fleshy finger pulled back his left eyelid and Harbinger's face crept closer.

"But all that doesn't matter for the moment. What I want to know is this. Can you tell me who you are, and what happened to you? Don't think I'm being impertinent, but we often get a slight touch of amnesia in cases like yours. Hardly ever permanent, but we must be sure."

"Yes, of course." Bill pulled himself up the bed and nodded. "My name is Bill Irwin. I'd been away from home and got back to my flat early in the morning. There was a man in the bedroom; a burglar, I suppose. I didn't see his face, but he hit me with something. When I came round the bell was ringing and there were two policemen at the front door. I thought they must have come about the burglary, but they told me that Mary—that's my wife—that she was dead. She'd been knocked over by a lorry in Yorkshire." His words came out in a rush. "After that I must have blacked out again."

"Yes, a terrible shock, and I'm very sorry about it, old man." Harbinger frowned. "But tell me, Mr. Irwin, can you remember what happened—what you were doing before you got back to the flat?"

"Before that?" Bill closed his eyes. The question was quite unimportant. Mary was dead, that was all that mattered. She'd stepped out in front of a lorry and the last time he'd seen her they'd quarrelled because he hadn't wanted her to go to Felcliff.

"Yes, where were you before you came home, Mr. Irwin? What were you doing?" Harbinger's voice seemed to come from the end of a long passage.

"I'd been away for some time, I think." Bill struggled to push back the days. The Dormobile bucketing over the rough Pennine roads. The early morning walks and the hiss of the Calor gas stove mingling with the sizzle of frying bacon. The click of the typewriter and the pages mounting into a thick pile on the desk. He'd always enjoyed that. Even if he had little faith in what he was writing, the mere sight of its physical growth never failed to give him pleasure.

But this book! The book which he'd gone away to try and finish! The book which Max Mayer had said could be his best after he'd looked at the outline! No, for some reason he hadn't enjoyed watching it grow, for somehow it hadn't seemed to have anything to do with him at all. As he sat at the typewriter, it was almost as though somebody's arms had been stretched over his shoulders and another person's fingers had rattled busily over the keys.

"Yes, I'd been away for almost a week," he said. "My wife had had to go to Yorkshire on business and I was having difficulty in finishing my last novel. I just took our shooting brake and toured about. I've got it fitted up with a bed and a desk, you see. I left on the Wednesday and I was away for—" He shook his head. "Just how long have I been here, Doctor?"

"Let me see." Harbinger consulted his watch. "Yes, four days and two hours almost to the minute. You were admitted here on the morning of the eleventh suffering from concussion and extreme nervous shock. Taken a very nasty knock on the head, and the X-ray showed that you have a slight condition of osteoporosis. I won't be technical, though. It merely means that your skull is weaker than normal, and the blow had more effect on the cerebral fluid than it would have done in most cases. Nothing to worry about and no lasting damage done, I'm happy to say. You should be back to your old self in no time."

His old self! Whatever had that been? It was rubbish in any case. After what they'd told him as he'd staggered across the hall of the flat, nothing could ever be the same. Bill watched Harbinger nod to the nurse and she opened the door. A thin, nondescript man in his early twenties came in. He had a notebook in his hand and looked slightly embarrassed.

"Ah, yes, this is Sergeant Hicks from the local police station. He wants to have a few words with you." Harbinger might have been making the introduction in the cheery, smoke-filled atmosphere of a saloon bar or a golf club. "I didn't let him come in till I was sure you were fit to talk.

"All right, Sergeant, you can have five minutes."

"Thank you, Doctor." Hicks pulled up a chair beside the bed. "Good morning, Mr. Irwin," he said. "I'm sorry to bother you when you've been so ill, but there are one or two points the inspector asked me to clear up. You don't mind, do you, sir?"

"No, of course not. You mean about the burglary, I suppose."

"The burglary?" If anything Hicks looked even younger and his expression became more embarrassed. "No, sir, we just want to run through your movements before you came home on the morning of the accident."

"My movements!" Bill struggled to remember. "No, I don't know, Sergeant," he said. "I honestly don't know." That was true enough. He had pictures of narrow roads winding in front of him, of moorland slopes and little hills and villages, of turning the car across a hump-backed bridge, of stopping to buy provisions, but none of the pictures fitted into any sequence. "I was touring almost at random, you see. Stopping whenever I found a place where I thought I could work and where it was possible to park the car for the night."

"Quite so, sir." Hicks made a neat note in his book. "Mr. Mayer, your publisher, told us that you would probably have done that. At any rate we know that by the tenth you had finished your novel and posted it off to him. That's correct, isn't it, sir?"

"Yes, I suppose so." He had a recollection of a pillarbox standing beside a village green and there was a line of brown hills in the distance. He seemed to remember that the package had been just small enough to force through the slot and he had heard it thud hollowly as it reached the bottom, but he couldn't really be sure. Hell, he couldn't really be sure about anything!

"Yes, we can confirm that, sir. Mr. Mayer told us that he received the typescript all safe and sound on the eleventh. But it's your journey back that we're really interested in. Did you by any chance drive home by way of Felcliff, the place where your wife was . . . ?"

"Where my wife was killed." Tucked away, far back in his mind, there was something he had to remember, but it just wouldn't come. All he could remember was the flick of the windscreen wipers, the wet road winding on through the headlights, and the hammering sound from the broken exhaust.

"No, I wouldn't have gone near Felcliff," he said. "It would have been miles out of my way. Besides, as far as I can remember, I didn't think she would still be there."

"I see, sir." Hicks made another note in his book. "And now, about this burglar you think hit you. We've been over the place with a fine-tooth comb and I'm afraid we haven't found a trace of any intruder. No sign of breaking and entering and, from what your daily woman tells us, no valuables appear to be missing."

"But there was somebody there. I saw him just before he hit me." Bill struggled to pull himself further up the bed. There suddenly seemed to be nothing more important in the world than to make Hicks believe his story.

"Yes, I know there was somebody there. I heard a sound behind me and I started to turn round. I saw his boots and trousers. The trousers looked like blue rubber in the light. He had a leather glove on his hand and I think he was holding some kind of wrench."

"Just a minute, Sergeant." Harbinger's fingers groped for his pulse. "Mr. Irwin has had a nasty blow and the devil of a shock, and imagination plays us queer tricks sometimes.

"Now, old boy, what seems to have happened is this. You came into the bedroom and stumbled against the rug by the dressing table; you'd been drinking pretty heavily, hadn't you? You fell and caught your head against the bedroom scales—they found blood on them. Approximately three hours later you came round, but were still in a state of concussion. You opened the door and found the police outside. They had come to tell you about the—the accident, though you didn't know that of course. You remember that much?"

"Yes, I remember that part of it." Bill closed his eyes and he could see exactly how it had been. The shiny dial of the scales in front of him with blood caked on the white enamel. The light still on in the bedroom and something like a mallet beating against his forehead. And then the bell had started to ring. At first he had thought it was just imagination, something to do with the dull blows in the head, but it had gone on ringing and ringing and at last he had got up and dragged himself to the door.

And they had been so kind. Two big fatherly men, just the type to break bad news. At first they had stood and gaped at him, incredulity mingling with the pity on their faces, and then an arm had gone round his shoulders.

"But you're hurt, sir—badly hurt. Come in and sit down now, and tell us what happened. What's that? You say there was a burglar—he hit you? Harry, take a look round and then ring the station. Tell 'em to send an ambulance over.

"What's that you say, sir? We've got over very quickly? Well, I'm sorry, Mr. Irwin, but I'm afraid we didn't come over about the burglar. As it happens we've got some bad news for you. Don't know if I should really be telling you now, but you'll have to know sooner or later. Last night at Felcliff—an accident, I'm sorry to say—your wife stepped out in front of a lorry—instantaneous death—couldn't have suffered at all . . .

You all right, sir? Hurry 'em up with that blasted ambulance, Harry."

The kindly face faded, the room started to spin, the blows of the mallet quickened, and he heard his own voice shouting, "No, no, no, I don't believe you." Blackness again.

"Yes," he said. "I remember all that, but there was a man in the bedroom. I know I'd had a lot to drink, but I saw him and I didn't fall. Sergeant, you must believe that I saw him."

"All right, we believe you. Easy, old boy, just take it easy." Something glinted in Harbinger's hand. "Sorry, Sergeant, but that's all I'm allowing for the time being. I think there'll be a great improvement tomorrow.

"Now, beddy byes for you, my old son." He felt the tiny stab of a needle in his arm and sleep came.

2

And everybody had been so extraordinarily kind. Sister Angus and Nurse Jackson had worn sad, proud smiles of farewell as he walked out of the ward; nannie and nursemaid saying good-bye to the young master, just off to his first term at prep school. Dr. Harbinger had beamed at him like the wicked uncle who has "knocked about a bit," and pumped his hand up and down. "Well, that's all we can do for you for the time being, old chap. Come back and see me in a fortnight, and don't bother about those blank spots in your memory. They'll fill themselves in all right, given time. Take another holiday, as I said, and try to forget everything. It may sound an Irishism, but very often forgetting is the best aid to memory."

Yes, all of them had been so kind. Bob Lefton had been waiting to drive him home. Good old Bob, as he liked to think of himself. Possibly the best literary agent in London and certainly one of its most tactful citizens. He could still see the slow, friendly smile curling up the little grey moustache and the nod that meant—"Don't try to talk about it—know how you must feel—know what you've been through. All my sympathy—terrible business—poor Mary." Though he felt as physically fit as he'd ever done, Bob had helped him into the car, insisted on wrapping a rug round his legs, and driven back at a steady twenty-five miles an hour as though he were a nervous dowager.

And at the flat more kindness. His sister, who had come up from Cornwall, tilting his face to the light and shaking her head. "Oh, my poor Bill—my poor, poor boy. What a shock you must have had! I do feel so terribly for you, though Mary and I never really got on." That was true enough. They'd had nothing in common and disliked each other at first glance. Anne's life was devoted to children and dogs and piles of knitting and the preparation of dull wholesome meals and Mary had probably never darned a sock in her life. "No, it would be hypocrisy to pretend that I liked her, but I'm so very, very sorry. Still, you're young, aren't you? Only thirty-two. There's plenty of time to start a new life. You will come and stay with us at Trebovir, won't you? Promise me that, darling."

And when Anne had gone, more kindness from Mrs. Carver, the daily help, though there was no attempt at stoicism on her part. "I've brought you these roses, Mr. Irwin. Yes, I thought you would like them. The missus always loved white roses, didn't she? I used to say that she was like a rose herself sometimes. Oh, the poor, poor missus; to think that it's less than three weeks ago since it happened. When I was doing the bedroom yesterday I could almost see her sitting there by the dressing table. I was as fond of her as of my own daughter . . ." It had taken him a month's back pay and three sizeable gin and tonics to stifle Mrs. Carver's grief.

Even the police had been kind. Shortly after Mrs. Carver left, Sergeant Hicks had arrived, bringing his superior with him. Inspector Carne was a tall, unprepossessing man with a narrow foxy face which was almost hidden by an enormous moustache, but he had gone out of his way to be civil.

"Now, sir, about this burglar whom you said you saw—who

you said hit you with some kind of wrench. We're very sorry, Mr. Irwin, but we haven't been able to find a trace of him. There's nothing missing, as far as we know. No drawers or cupboards have been forced open. We found no fingerprints . . ." In vain Bill told him that the man had worn gloves and that no drawers or cupboards could have been forced, since none were locked, but Carne obviously considered the figure he had seen was a mere product of his imagination.

"But there's one small point that you might help us to clear up, Mr. Irwin. The hotel receptionist told the Felcliff police that your wife said she was catching the midnight train to London and would be coming straight back here. She mentioned that taxis were sometimes difficult to find at King's Cross in the early morning, and hoped she would get one all right. Now, I suppose you didn't telephone her at Felcliff, sir, and say that you would be back here when she arrived."

"No, no, of course not. I'd planned to be away for at least another two days. I finished my book much sooner than I expected. I . . ." Once again Bill's memory sank into vacuum.

"I see, sir. You finished your work before schedule and decided to come home." Carne's eyes regarded him gravely above the flowing moustache. "But what puzzles me is how your wife hoped to get into the flat if there was nobody here. We didn't find any key amongst her belongings."

"What! But that's impossible, Inspector. She must have had a key on her. My wife was a most methodical woman. She'd have been as likely to have gone out without her shoes as without a key."

"Quite so, sir, that's what Mr. Allan Wayne, her employer, told us. But we needn't let it worry us too much, I think. Her handbag was completely shattered by the impact and the key may have been thrown down a drain. Also that stretch of road was very muddy—it's used by lorries working on the harbour project and the tire of a passing vehicle might have picked it up after the accident and carried it miles away." The policeman opened his brief case and pulled out a grey folder.

"Now, sir, as you were unable to attend the inquest, I expect you'd like to have a look at a transcript of the evidence."

"Yes, of course I want to see it." Bill took the file from him and opened it. The bare, official, dispassionate statement of the end of a life, with the arms of the South Riding Constabulary neatly embossed on the first sheet, and the evidence laid out like the plan of a novel—exposition, body, *finis*.

"Mrs. Irwin had worked as my personal secretary for over three years . . ." That was Allan Wayne, of course. Big, jolly Jumbo Wayne, as his friends called him, though there was nothing elephantine or ponderous about Allan, and the nickname was quite inappropriate. A loud bouncing man who looked as though his body had been blown up like a rubber tire and would burst if you pricked him.

"Since September the first, Mrs. Irwin and I had been travelling frequently between London and Felcliff in connection with the Felcliff Harbour Development Scheme which is in the hands of my company, Star Construction . . ." *My company!* Lucky Jumbo! He'd done all right for himself. Married the boss's stepdaughter and shot up from a fifteen-pound-a-week clerk in the drawing office to fifteen thousand a year.

"Mrs. Irwin was to have returned to London with some papers concerning the demolition works on the afternoon train of the tenth. She told me that she was unable to do this, having some business at Felcliff to finish off, and would catch the night train instead. Her death has been a great personal loss to me, and on behalf of Star Construction I would like to say how much we regret that one of our lorries was the innocent cause of it."

So much for Jumbo. The hotel receptionist came next: Mrs. Kay Sommers, aged twenty-seven, widow. "Mrs. Irwin left the hotel at about eleven thirty p.m. to go to the station. She was returning to Felcliff on the following day and only had a handbag and a small overnight case with her. I offered to telephone for a taxi, as it was starting to rain slightly, but she said that she preferred to walk."

She preferred to walk! That was wrong somehow. The page seemed to blur under Bill's eyes as he read the sentence. Mary hated walking. He remembered a score of occasions when they had stood waiting for a cab rather than walk a couple of blocks. And it was starting to rain as well! Yes, there was something wrong here—very wrong. If only he could remember.

He craned over the page again and tried to imagine how it must have been. A deserted, dying town, just before midnight. Felcliff was dying all right, for most of its centre was being pulled down to make way for the new harbour and docks. Drizzle and mist drifting in from the sea. A red sign, Star Construction, glowing out on a crane that towered over the river, and Mary's heels click, click, clicking on towards the station. And just before the station? The glimpse of a clock moving on towards midnight, perhaps. The sound of a locomotive blowing off steam. A road junction that had to be crossed and in the distance, but coming closer, the rattle of a diesel engine. A foot off the pavement and . . .

"I was travelling at about twenty-five miles an hour." John Caplin, lorry driver, Flat 9, Ascayne House, 350 Briarhill Road, West Norwood, SE25.

"Visibility was only fair and the road surface greasy, but my vehicle is fitted with air brakes. I didn't see the lady—yes, I mean the deceased of course—until just before I hit her. She must have been standing behind the phone box at the junction of North Cliff Road and Grand Parade. She just seemed to appear in front of me like. I jammed on my brakes and tried to pull out, but there was nothing I could do to avoid her.

"Yes, I had been on the road for five hours since leaving our London depot, but I was not unduly tired."

So much for John Caplin, though a Mr. James Millar, M.SC., M.I.Mech.E., transport manager of Star Construction, stated that he had been in their employ for two years and had a clean licence. There was also a note from a police mechanic certifying that his vehicle, a Leyland lorry, AVK 995, had been loaded well within its capacity and was in excellent mechanical order.

So much for that. The coroner had recorded a verdict of accidental death, though he stated that he deplored the practice of placing obstructions near important road junctions. He recommended that the telephone booth in question should be removed, or at least placed further back from the curb.

Yes, so much for everything. Bill closed the folder on his wife's death and held it out to Carne.

"No, you keep it, sir. We have another copy." The policeman stood up and tightened the belt of his coat. "And I think that's the lot, Mr. Irwin, though of course I'd like to offer you my personal sympathy. If we should come up with anything to substantiate your story about the burglar, we'll naturally get in touch with you.

"No, please don't bother to show us out, sir. The sergeant and I know our way." A handshake and a smile, a little nod from Hicks, two pairs of well-polished boots moved away and then paused by the door. Carne's eyes stared back at him above the silly moustache.

"As I'm here, Mr. Irwin, there's just one more thing I think I should ask you, and I hope you won't feel I'm being impertinent. The coroner recorded a verdict of accidental death and we've no quarrel with that. All the same I wondered—just wondered—if your wife had been under any emotional strain lately. If there is any chance that she deliberately . . ."

"You mean could she have committed suicide? Did she throw herself in front of that lorry on purpose?" Bill shook his head. The very idea was ludicrous. People as ambitious as Mary didn't kill themselves, though in some cases the opposite might be true. Though he'd loved her very much he'd never had the slightest doubts about her ruthlessness or her ambition. Besides, there was another reason against suicide; the best reason of them all.

"My wife was a Catholic," he said.

"I see, sir. Then that clears that up. I hope you didn't mind my asking. Good-bye again, Mr. Irwin." The door closed and he was alone at last.

And now there were letters to be opened. Notes of condolence mainly, though others had been posted before she died.

From Allan Wayne. Thick, creamy paper with the scarlet crest of the Star Construction Company showing a tall building with a crane beside it and a star above the crane. The heading showed that the London office ran to fifteen telephone lines and there were branches in ten other cities. "Dear Bill . . . My deepest sympathy—must meet soon—terrible loss—can't tell you how very sorry I am—on firm's business—no obligation of course—possible to work out some form of compensation . . ."

Damn Jumbo! Damn him for even mentioning money at this stage. Bill had always resented, even hated Mary working for Jumbo, though he knew it had been necessary. He could almost hear her voice during one of their regular rows on the subject. "Darling, you're jealous—jealous of Jumbo. Silly old Jumbo who doesn't even know how to look at a woman. He's just a meal ticket, Bill, a way to pay the rent."

No, Jumbo Wayne hadn't exactly paid the rent, but there was no doubt that Mary's salary had been necessary for her ambitions: the two cars, the Dior suits, the mink, the parties. The horrible, dull parties which he'd hated and had seemed to come round as regularly as clockwork. The next letter confirmed his thoughts. A bare, official note from his bank, containing no condolence, but stating that their joint account was overdrawn £312 . 1s . 9d at the close of the day's business.

So many letters! From Mary's brother in Ireland—from Michael Seaton with whom he had collaborated on a television play that nobody had wanted to produce—from Mary's friends, Joan and Laura—the electricity bill—the rates demand note—from an aunt he hadn't seen in years—from . . . ?

No, he couldn't place this one at first. "Number 3, Monk's Close, Mayfair," and dated two days before the accident. Rather slanting, spidery writing which could have been written by a very old or feeble person.

Dear Mr. Irwin,

You and I have never met, but under the circumstances it is high time that we did. While my husband is at Felcliff I am staying with my stepfather at the above address. Would you be kind enough to telephone me here so that we can arrange an appointment.

RUTH WAYNE

Ruth Wayne! That was Jumbo's wife, but what on earth could she want to see him about? Somehow, far back in his mind, he felt that he should know the answer, but his memory was still in a vacuum. She was wrong about one thing, of course. They had met at some party Jumbo had given last year. They had only spoken a few words, but he remembered her well. A very dark girl who would have been beautiful if it were not for the pain and bitterness in her face. Tall, too, probably, though he could only guess that, for she had sat in a wheel chair with a rug over her knees. A hunting accident had done it, he seemed to remember. The horse had fallen on top of her and left her paralyzed from the waist down.

He lifted the telephone and then replaced it as he saw the next letter on the pile. Before he called Ruth Wayne he would see what Max Mayer, his publisher, had to say.

As always he was struck by the layout of Max's correspondence. Though he was technically the firm's fiction editor, the love of his life was typography and his secretary seemed to share it. The letter looked as though it had been printed rather than typed, and there was a serious attempt at justification in the right-hand margin. The italic signature would have looked more at home on a diploma or an illuminated scroll.

The first half of the letter was as he had expected. "Can't tell you how sorry I am—when I lost my own wife—if one can only have faith—Time, the great healer . . ."

So much for sympathy. Soon Max came down to business ". . . hate to bother you at this stage, but it is my duty as your publisher to do so." That was pretty high-flown, even for Max. *As your father confessor it is my duty to warn you!" "As your medical adviser I must tell you that if you persist in this manner of life . . ."*

But just what was it that Max had to bother him about?

"As you know, we are intending to bring out your new book *Members' Enclosure* next June. I have read the first draft with great interest, and feel that we should have a talk about it as soon as possible. The first three-quarters or so, up to the beginning of Chapter 12, in fact, is as good as anything you have done, but after that a marked deterioration seems to have set in. The ending, for example, strikes me as being quite out of character, and also completely out of tune with the rest of the plot."

The end! Bill frowned at the letter for a moment and then with a sudden, convulsive gesture, screwed it up and threw it away from him. He lit a cigarette and dragged hard at it, trying to remember how it had been. Yes, he had finished the book all right. Sometime in the afternoon it was, with the car parked beside a little stream, and though the sun was bright, fine rain was driving across the moorland. He remembered looking at the wad of typescript on the desk, but feeling none of his usual pleasure as he slid the staples through it. He remembered how the package had rattled down into the roadside pillar-box as he finally managed to twist it through the slot, but there was something else which he just couldn't remember. Something a hundred times more important than any novel.

He got up from the table and stared at his face in the mirror by the window. Not a bad face; quite a handsome face, as Mary had often told him. A strong firm chin with a cleft in it, thick fair hair above a broad forehead, a straight nose, and blue eyes. Pale blue eyes, the very pale blue eyes that many murderers were said to have had.

No, not a bad face, but perhaps a crazy face. He turned away from the mirror and stared down at the crumpled sheet of paper on the floor. The face of a man who couldn't even remember the end of a book he had just written.

3

"In five minutes please, Miss Roebuck. Send Mr. Irwin up in exactly five minutes." Maximilian Mayer put down the telephone and crossed to the steel filing cabinet in the corner of his office, glancing anxiously at it, as though it were an extremely dangerous and unreliable piece of machinery; a bomb or booby-trap which might easily explode if he touched the wrong handle. His secretary had been away for a week, laid low with influenza, and he felt completely lost and helpless without her.

Now, just where had he put the damned thing? Very cautiously Mayer pulled open a drawer labelled "I to M" and then grinned with relief as he saw the wad of typescript. Yes, *"Members' Enclosure* . . . First rough draft of 65,000 words . . . William Irwin, 8, Riverside Court, s.w. 14." He carried it back to his desk, removing a sheet of notes which Jack Prout, his senior partner, had clipped to the title page as he did so. No, it wouldn't do for Irwin to look at them. By and large Prout had merely commented on style and minor anomalies of the plot, but his last remark read, "Chapter 12!!! Cor, stone the crows! Has he gone right round the bend?"

And quite possibly he had gone round the bend. Mayer had always thought Irwin was a rum sort of fellow and this seemed to confirm it. He flicked the book open at the offending chapter and shook his head sadly. This wasn't merely ill-constructed and badly written, but quite impossible. Irwin had published eight novels and should know his job by now. He must have realized just how bad it was.

Yes, a very rum fellow indeed. There had been no covering note with the typescript and he'd probably written the ending in that van which he'd fitted up as a travelling office-cum-bedroom. The girl on the reception desk had told Mayer that it had been posted somewhere in Derbyshire and the wrapping was torn as though the parcel had been forced into the box. She'd also had to pay one and threepence in extra postage. It was a wonder it had reached them at all, and there wouldn't be a copy either. Time and again he'd asked Irwin to take carbons, but he'd always said it was unnecessary for a first draft.

Yes, quite impossible. Mayer closed the book, feeling a slight twinge of heartburn left over from a large and exotic lunch, and leaned back in his chair. He was sorry about Mary Irwin's death, of course, though by all accounts she'd been an extravagant and over-ambitious woman. With American and translation rights, Irwin must make quite a lot of money, but she probably spent up to the hilt. That last party they gave would have set him back a bit. Over sixty guests, two hired waiters and enough champagne to swim in. The fat chap she worked for, Cain or Wayne, something like that, had got pretty high before it broke up. He'd monopolized Mary Irwin all the evening and kept leering at her as though she belonged to him. Irwin hadn't liked it either, Mayer had seen his expression as he watched them across the room, but possibly there was nothing he could do about it. His Mary was obviously a very headstrong little piece, and they needed her job to keep up their standard of living. She should have married someone like Wayne if she wanted to give parties of that sort every few months, run a couple of cars and sport a mink coat. A pretty woman, if you liked that slim elegant type, which Mayer didn't, but she must have given Irwin a lot of headaches.

He should be on his way up by now. Mayer glanced at his watch and laid the typescript neatly at the side of his desk. He wasn't looking forward to the interview one little bit. Slight amnesia following shock, the hospital had said. He'd have to go carefully with him. Point out the faults of the book as tactfully as possible and try not to cause any offence. The fellow's novels sold a steady eight thousand in hard covers alone, and though that didn't make him a gold mine he was still a pretty valuable piece of property. Yes, he'd be very, very careful.

"My dear chap, this is a pleasure. A great pleasure." Mayer bounded to his feet with a beam of welcome as Bill came through the doorway.

"Now, sit down and make yourself comfortable. It's extremely good of you to come and see me at this sad time. You know how I feel about your loss so I won't say any more." He squeezed Bill's arm and led him to a chair. The fellow really was looking bad, he thought. Not physically ill, perhaps, but pinched and haunted somehow, as though under terrible strain. He hoped he wouldn't go and dry up. The lending libraries practically queued for his stuff, and it would be a bit of a body blow if the firm lost him.

"Well, you're certainly looking much better than I expected," he said. "Can't keep a good man down, eh?"

"Thank you." Bill smiled back. "I feel fit enough physically. It's just this . . ."

"Yes, just that wretched amnesia. They told me about it when I rang the hospital." Mayer nodded sympathetically. "It must be horrible, but I wouldn't worry too much, if I were you. Sure to pass in time. I remember a similar thing happened to another of our authors once. Cuthbut Spain it was, back in '55. The poor chap fell off a mountain in Wales and came round imagining himself . . ." He broke off hurriedly. This would never do. Not only damned rude—Spain had imagined himself to be Philip II and was still in the bin, weeping for his lost Armada—but time-wasting as well. There was a string quartet at the Wigmore Hall that evening which Mayer didn't want to miss, and he hoped to leave the office early.

"But I mustn't bore you with reminiscences. I'm quite sure that you'd like to get our business over and be left in peace." He pulled across Bill's typescript.

"Yes, here we are. *Members Only*—sorry, *Members' Enclosure.* A good book, as I said on the telephone, a very good book indeed! Up to a point, that is." He squinted slightly as he flicked through the pages. "Yes, up to—where are we now? Yes, up to the start of Chapter 12, this is as good as anything you've done, and that's saying a great deal."

"But you don't like the end?" Bill watched the busy little fingers turning the pages. He had written them less than three weeks ago, but it might have been a hundred years.

"No, I don't like it all." Once again heartburn fluttered in Mayer's chest and he stifled a belch. "You see, up to Chapter 12, you've written a very amusing light comedy about this couple, Roger and Jane, who both think the other is being unfaithful and do a bit of amateur detective work to try and prove their suspicions. Not an entirely original theme, perhaps, but you've treated it very well and there are some excellent situations and dialogue. The side plots are good too. That business at Roger's office, about who will be taken on the board of directors, and the brother-in-law who is always changing his job; yes, quite a Micawber figure you've got there.

"By the way, did you deliberately make some of the situations autobiographical?"

"Autobiographical? Why on earth should you say that, Max?"

"Well, there seem to be a few suggestions of it. The honeymoon in Ibiza, for example. I think that ties up with you and Mary."

"Yes, of course, but there was no real reason for Ibiza, except that it's always easier to write about somewhere you know."

"Ah, quite so." Mayer nodded approvingly. "I wish more authors realized that. We had a chap in here only last week, as it happens. Wanted us to commission him to do a book on the Amazon, and it turned out that he'd never been farther than a cruise to the West Indies.

"But surely there are other things as well. Your hero, this fellow Roger, for instance, writes in his spare time and he buys his house with the advance from an American book club. That happened in your case, I think."

"You know perfectly well it did, Max, but so what?" Bill

frowned at Mayer across the desk. What on earth was the old boy driving at? They'd known each other for years, and Max knew perfectly well that he always used autobiographical details if they would fit into the plot.

"Oh, nothing, nothing at all. Don't know why I even mentioned it." Mayer flicked on through the typescript. Irwin really was in a bad way, he thought. A bag of nerves and ready to take offence at the slightest thing. He'd have to go very easy with him.

"But to get back to the structure of the story," he said. "You have the main situation of this married couple who both begin to think that the other is being unfaithful. The rest of the characters know this is untrue and the reader is clearly told that it is untrue. So why do you have to go and change it in the last chapter?"

"The last chapter?" Bill leaned forward. Before they discussed the book there was something he wanted to know. "Max," he said, "a few days ago the police came round here and asked you some questions about me. What exactly did they say?"

"Oh, that!" Mayer silently cursed his fate. He was hoping to go home and change after leaving the office, and in less than two and a half hours the Kurt Fischer Quartet would be tuning up. "Yes, a couple of them called on Tuesday, I think it was. There was a sergeant who looked about sixteen and didn't say a word and an inspector . . . No, I can't remember his name."

"Carne?"

"Yes, that's it, Carne. 'A vulgar person who appeared to be all moustache,' if I may quote from *Diary of a Nobody*. It was purely routine. Because of your loss of memory they wanted to try and piece your movements together, and wondered if we could help. Quite unnecessary, if you ask me, and everything will fill itself in, given time. I merely told them that you had been touring in the north of England and that we had received your typescript from a place in Derbyshire.

"And now, about this ending." He looked at his watch and pushed the typescript across to Bill. "Up to nine-tenths of the way through the book you've been building up to a grand reconciliation scene. Everything else has resolved itself; the office strife is over and the brother-in-law has at last got a job which pleases him. All the reader wants now is for Jane and Roger to realize their folly and make things up.

"But then what happens?" Mayer frowned as he studied Bill's face. Haunted really was the word to describe it; pinched, frightened somehow. He struggled to concentrate on the plot. "Yes, without any valid reason being given, you suddenly send your hero, Roger, off to Paris. There he gets maudlin drunk, becomes convinced that Jane has been unfaithful to him, and goes to bed with the first whore he meets. Completely out of character, you know. Quite out of tune with the rest of the story."

"Yes, I can see that." Bill stared at the typescript. Like all his first drafts it was untidy, misspelt and underpunctuated, but somehow it seemed quite different from the others. It might have been written by another person, and he couldn't recognize a single paragraph of the final chapter. "And what does he do after that, Max?" he said.

"After the whore episode?" Mayer's frown deepened. "But you know yourself, Bill. After all, you wrote it."

"No, I'm sorry, but I don't know, Max. That's the point. I may have written it, but I can't remember anything about the ending."

"I see." Mayer reached for his cigarettes. He'd been trying to cut down to three a day after meals, but he suddenly wanted one very badly. Had that visit from the police been as routine as it appeared, he wondered? After all, the chap had lost his memory. Almost a whole day had gone out of his life. He might have done anything and forgotten about it completely; anything at all. No, that was ridiculous. He was letting his imagination run away with him. All the same . . .

"In your last chapter," he said, "Roger comes back from

Paris firmly convinced that his wife has been cuckolding him for years. He arrives home in the early hours of the morning and goes up to the bedroom where she is asleep. But surely you don't need me to tell you any more?"

"Yes, I'm afraid I do, Max." The pages blurred under Bill's eyes so that he could hardly read them and he felt trickles of sweat running down from his armpits. "I know it sounds incredible, but I honestly don't remember."

"Very well." Mayer lit his cigarette and inhaled deeply. "The ending is very abrupt and, like the prostitute business, quite out of keeping with the rest of the story. For some reason which you don't explain, the wife has an ornamental dagger on her dressing table. Your so-called hero picks it up and kills her."

4

But could he have written that? Could he really have done so? He'd always thought of himself as a light, satirical writer, keeping tension down to the minimum, looking for atmosphere rather than action and never overdrawing a character. And as Max had told him, reading out the more outrageous passages to drive home his points, the ending of this book had not only been out of character, but quite ludicrous. A reasonable, ultra-respectable, pipe-smoking Englishman who, on the vague suspicion that his wife might—only might—have been unfaithful to him, had thrown up his job, dashed off to Paris and, after an evening of self-pity and alcoholic introspection, had gone home with the first drab who accosted him. Rubbish!

And why—why—why couldn't he even remember writing it? Everything else was falling into place now. He had been having trouble in finishing the book, and Star Construction had told Mary that she would have to be in Felcliff for the first two weeks of the month. It had seemed obvious that he should go away and try to work things out.

Yes, that was clear enough now. He'd kept to a rough itinerary so that Mrs. Carver could forward his mail, and he'd rung Mary up on alternate days, sometimes at Felcliff and once or twice in London when she'd had to go back for plans and documents. He could remember the route he'd taken as well: Chester, Keswick, Appleby and a place called Sedale in the Peak District. And at Sedale, something had happened and his memory had gone blank.

But what could it have been? Just what could have made him sit down and write that crazy, incompetent ending? As he walked through the evening streets, already filled with office workers on their way home, the final pages of the typescript burned in front of his eyes. That stolid, respectable man whom he'd named Roger Haynes creeping upstairs to his wife's bedroom, picking up a dagger, which in all conscience was an unlikely thing to find on a dressing table, and bringing it down on her sleeping body.

Yes, ludicrous! And the last passage was just plain crazy. How did it go again?

Roger knelt down beside the body of the woman he had killed and he was tired—terribly tired. Somebody else would have to take care of things now. Somebody else—Uncle Mark probably—would have to pay the boys' school fees. Somebody else would have to see about selling the house. He was just too tired to bother any more. "Oh, my dear," he said, staring down at the face which seemed even more beautiful in death. "Oh, darling, come back and help me . . ."

God! Shades of—no, complete cribs from Hemingway, Winifred Holtby and Hugh Walpole! He clutched the typescript a little tighter under his arm and, as he did so, felt something rustle in his pocket. The letter with the Mayfair address which he had read before calling Max. "You and I have never met, but under the circumstances it is high time that we did." He turned into a phone booth, fumbling for a 3d bit and pulling out the letter. MAYfair 1110, a very nice combination for a private number, but this one belonged to the owner of several million pounds. In the darkening sky above Trafalgar Square the electric signs were coming up, and far away towards the river, from the top of a crane over some unfinished building possibly, he could see the title and motto of his wife's firm STAR CONSTRUCTION—UP ON TIME.

"Mayvair double vun, vun, zero." The voice of a foreign maid probably. "Sir Norman Star's residence. Vill you hold on please, sir, and I vill see if Mrs. Vayne is at home." There was a click and the line went dead for a moment as though they had been cut off. Bill waited, watching the cars and buses moving jerkily down the Strand; the crowds pouring into Charing Cross station; a thickset man with a heavy arrogant face that reminded him of a side of uncooked ham who peered at him through the window and then marched heavily away as though looking for another booth.

"Mr. Irwin? This is Ruth Wayne." Even on the telephone he could recognize the hint of physical pain in her voice. "I'm glad you rang, Mr. Irwin. Allan told me about the death of your wife and I'd like to say how very sorry I am for you."

"Thank you, Mrs. Wayne. Thank you very much. Actually I'm sorry not to have rung as soon as I got your letter, but I've been ill."

"Yes, I heard that too. But don't worry about the letter, Mr. Irwin. It's no longer of any importance and it was foolish of me to have sent it in the first place. I would be grateful if you would try to forget that you received it." Her tone sounded guarded and he sensed that she was not alone.

"But just a moment, Mrs. Wayne. I think you ought to tell me what the letter was about. You worded it pretty strongly, you know."

"Yes, I do know that and, as I said, it was stupid of me to have sent it." She broke off for a moment and Bill heard something rattle. A glass? A teacup? Shaky pain-racked fingers playing with china ornaments on a dressing table?

"Mr. Irwin, please believe me that, in the present circumstances, it would be far better for both of us if you could forget that letter."

"And, as I said, I'm afraid I can't forget it, Mrs. Wayne. You wrote and implied that you had something important to tell me. I think I have a right to know what it is."

"Yes, I suppose you have that right." Another pause, another rattle and then complete resignation in her voice. "Very well, Mr. Irwin. Could you call round here at about eleven o'clock tomorrow? Thank you. Until eleven then."

In the present circumstances? Bill put down the phone and stepped out of the booth. It was quite dark now with a hint of fog drifting up from the river and already the home-going crowds seemed to be thinning out. Everybody going home, but he had no home to go to. The thought of that empty flat was suddenly repellent to him, and almost automatically he turned into a saloon bar at the corner and ordered a whisky.

. . . in the present circumstances, it would be far better for both of us if you could forget that letter. The only circumstances that had changed had been Mary's death, and, though his whole mind fought against it, Bill was beginning to feel that he knew what Ruth Wayne wanted to say to him. He sat down at a table in one of the alcoves and stared across the room. It was furnished in mahogany and red plush, with two brass nymphs standing at either end of the counter and between them a pert little barmaid who looked as though she should be wrapped up in tissue paper with "Happy Christmas, boys" written on the label. Above her head an oil painting of some former proprietor wearing Masonic dress glowered down on the proceedings.

It was the first drink he'd had since his breakdown, and at the second sip the whisky began to go to his head. The place was still comfortably full, though like the street it was beginning to thin out as city workers headed for home. Men with bowler hats and dark suits—men with umbrellas and brief cases—men who talked about the weather and their gardens and the end of the cricket season—men with wives and homes and a future—men who had no connection with him at all. He unfolded his paper, determined for five minutes at least to put all thoughts of Mary's death or what he suspected Ruth Wayne had to tell him out of his mind. A bad rail accident in the Midlands—a slight fall on Wall Street—the death of an Italian statesman—the marriage of a very minor film actress . . .

He started to turn the page, and as he did so the floor creaked, a heavy body in a thick black suit lowered itself into a chair and the arrogant, sagging face he had seen from the phone booth grinned at him across the table.

"Evening." The owner of the face took a deep gulp at his pint of beer and smacked his lips with every sign of satisfaction. "Yes, very, very good, as always. This is one of the few houses in London where one can still get a really well-kept glass of Scotch ale. A foul evening, eh, Mr. Irwin, and likely to get still fouler by the look of it."

"You know me?" Bill started slightly. There was "copper" written in every line of that craggy body and those hanging jowls.

"Yes, in a way. Like I know the Prime Minister and Greta Garbo. Seen your picture on the back of a book jacket and I never forget a face." He opened his jacket to show the glint of a watch chain across his vast stomach.

"I've read one of your books as it happens. Last year it was, when we went to Spain. Hate going abroad myself, but the wife puts her foot down sometimes; foolish woman in many ways. I got badly sunburned, of course, and had to spend a week in bed. The only book in English that I could find was one of yours. Can't remember the title, but it was about a chap who tries to take over his father's business and comes to a pretty sticky end."

"Yes, *Ram in the Thicket*." Bill grinned to himself at the thought of that well-draped body ever being exposed to the sun and he could almost picture the man's holiday. Outlandish food which didn't agree with him and drinks he didn't enjoy— slow, miserable walks beside the surf while his wife shopped

or wrote innumerable picture postcards—a constant count of
the hours to the happy day when he could return to his cro-
nies, his job, and his dark, gloomy office—even an approach
with a quoit or beach ball to another lonely figure in the hope
of killing monotony: "Would you care to have a game, sir?"
The agony of sunburn might have proved a slight relief from
boredom.

"Did you enjoy the book?" he asked.

"No, not especially, but it helped to pass the time. Outrageous what the dagoes asked for it, though! Ordinary paper
edition clearly marked half a crown and they had the imperti-
nence to charge four and six."

"Yes, I know that. I only wish I got royalties on those prices."

"You mean you don't?" The man took another swig of beer
and started to ram tobacco into a short blackened pipe. "You
chaps should form some sort of trade union to look after your
rights. By the way, you know who I am, of course?"

"No, I'm afraid I don't." Bill shook his head, though somehow he felt he should remember the face. Pictures in newspapers or magazines? A flash on the television screen?

"Really!" The smile changed to a slightly petulant frown.
"You've got a very poor memory, Mr. Irwin, though it's some
time since I was in the public eye. I'm Pode—Superintendent
George Pode."

"Yes, of course I remember." The pictures clicked into
position. The man's heavy face beaming out under newspaper
headlines—"Smart work by Inspector Pode"—the big body
marching purposefully up the steps to the murder house with
a group of minions at its heels: "Supt. George Pode states that
he is confident of making an arrest in the near future."

Following retirement, Pode's name had figured in a series
of self-laudatory articles in one of the Sunday newspapers:
PODE OF THE C.I.D.—PODE OF THE FLYING SQUAD—MURDER-
ERS I HAVE BROUGHT TO BOOK by Supt. George Pode. The
complete modesty in his style had been rather endearing.

The Commissioner's face was pale with worry. "It's up to you now, George," he said. The moment I came into the room I knew the type of man I was up against. "Don't worry, lads," the desk sergeant said. "Now they've put Mr. Pode on the case we'll see some action. No, the Super won't let no grass grow under his boots."

"Yes, it was stupid of me not to know you at once." Bill grinned apologetically. "I've had rather a lot of worry recently and my memory is a bit hazy."

"Yes, so I've heard and there's no need to apologize." Pode's pipe was filled to his satisfaction at last and he lit it, blowing a cloud of rank, acrid smoke across the table. "Sorry about your wife's death by the way, and then there was that wretched business of the burglar, wasn't there?"

"You know about that?"

"Oh yes, I keep my ears open, even if I have retired." He took another deep gulp of beer. "Talked to Mike Carne, as it happens. He was one of my boys in the old days. I taught him everything he knows, though he seems to have forgotten most of it. He didn't believe your story about the burglar, did he?"

"No, he didn't believe me. But what about you, Mr. Pode? Do you honestly think I could have imagined it all? I mean I can remember the details so clearly: the boots, the dark trousers which looked blue in the light, the hand in the glove and the thing like a wrench coming down."

"I've no idea, old boy. Not my case and all I've got to go on is what young Carne told me. All the same, if it were my case . . ." Pode paused and blew his nose with quite unnecessary violence.

"If it were my case, I think I might be inclined to give you the benefit of the doubt. No, no, let me finish, Mr. Irwin." He raised a great, gnarled hand as Bill tried to break in.

"Carne doesn't believe you, because there were no signs of breaking and entering and nothing is missing from the flat. Well, perhaps he's wrong. Perhaps something is missing which your wife left there on her last visit to London and which neither you nor the maid know about. That's just supposition, of course, but the circumstances of your blackout interest me as well. At about seven forty-five in the morning the local coppers come round to break the news of the accident to you. When you open the door to them you are bleeding from a cut on the head but, apart from the story about the burglar, you seem pretty rational. Then the sergeant tells you your wife is dead and you pass straight out. A mental blackout, in fact, caused by nervous shock and not the blow." Pode finished his beer and frowned at the empty glass.

"But as you're picking my brains, what about getting me a refill, Bill? You don't mind my using your Christian name, do you? I never could stand on ceremony."

"No, of course not." Bill crossed to the bar, feeling hope for the first time in days. At least somebody admitted the possibility that he might be telling the truth. No, hope was not the right word. Even as he carried the glasses back to the table he knew that what he felt was a mixture of hope and fear and dread. The burglar had been there all right, but what had happened at Sedale which he couldn't remember and what might he have done on that long journey home? Could he have knocked somebody down with the car, perhaps, and could this have driven it out of his mind?

"Superintendent," he said. Somehow he couldn't bring out "George." "In your experience, is it possible that a person could do something that was utterly repugnant to him and, after a brainstorm brought about by shock, alcohol, or what you like, completely forget about it?"

"In my experience, perfectly possible, though a lot of the head shrinkers would disagree with me. Cheers!" Pode raised his glass and drank deeply.

"Plenty of cases to back me up as well. Take Peter Fletcher of Ely, for example. He was a jobbing gardener; pleasant little man with no history of violence or insanity. He had a slight quarrel with his employer and beat him to death with a spade. Afterwards he drank a full bottle of Scotch and passed out.

Though they hanged him, I'm prepared to swear that he had no recollection of the murder. Then there was Maria Grey-wolf; a half-breed Sioux Indian. She stabbed and castrated her lover in an empty carriage of the b.m.t. railway in New York and honestly believed that she was attending a revivalist meeting at the time."

"Yes, I've read about her." As the old, self-opinionated voice droned on, a dozen unpleasant possibilities ran through Bill's mind.

"But to talk about the inquest on your wife for a moment." Pode fumbled in the musty depths of his pocket and produced a notebook. "I've been thinking about the case quite a lot, as it happens. Rather a hobby of mine these days, trying to read between the lines of inquests. Keeps the old brain active. Something very smelly there, you know."

"Smelly!" Bill's hand tightened round his glass. "Just what do you mean?"

"I mean everything about it, old boy; the whole setup. Midnight, deserted streets, her walking instead of taking a cab, mud on the road to account for the truck skidding and the phone booth conveniently placed by the junction. Was your wife the kind of woman to step off a curb without looking to see if the road was clear? Remember that those heavy diesels make quite a racket."

"No, she was always very careful." Bill didn't even have to consider to answer that one.

"Quite so. And you heard that the fellow had a record, I suppose? Damn good beer this!" Pode drank again and belched. Not a quiet ashamed belch as Max Mayer had made, but a great burst of air that shook his watch chain and reverberated around the room.

"Yes, the driver." He flicked through the notebook. "Here we are—John Caplin, aged forty-two, of Flat 9, Ascayne House, 350 Briarhill Road, West Norwood, SE25. He was up in front of the beak when he was seventeen for stealing a motor-cycle and got sent to a Borstal institution. When he was thirty he did three years for breaking and entering; no remission for good conduct either."

"But he was exonerated over the accident. The magistrate said that he couldn't possibly have avoided her."

"So he did, Bill, but what else could he say? The only witness was Mr. John Caplin himself. May I?" Pode's pipe had gone out and he reached over and helped himself to one of Bill's cigarettes.

"Thank you. Yes, a man with a record of dishonesty and a very glib story indeed which it is not possible to question. If it were my case, I think that I'd have a great deal to say to Mr. Caplin, you know."

"But why? She stepped right out in front of the truck. What else could he have done?" Bill struck a match and lit the cigarette for him.

"Yes, she stepped out in front of him. The magistrate said she did. The Felcliff police accept that she did. Mr. Caplin swears that she did. And it's not my case either. I'm just an old fossil with a hobby of reading between the lines of inquest reports. Must be toddling now, though." He finished the beer and hitched up his coat prior to departure.

"All the same, I don't mind betting that there's somebody who is very pleased that I'm not in charge of the case."

"Look, Mr. Pode, just what the hell are you driving at?" Once again Bill's hand tightened convulsively and he felt whisky spill from his glass and slop over the table. "My wife was killed in an accident."

"Yes, so they say, Bill, and don't pay any attention to me; just an old fossil, as I told you before." Pode stood up and grinned at him.

"And they are probably quite right. Smart lot of coppers at Felcliff, bright young coroner, open-and-shut case and it's nothing to do with me. All the same, if it were my business, old boy—if it were my case—then I wouldn't have started on the supposition that it was an accident." He brushed a spot of ash from his sleeve and put on his hat. It was far too small for him and looked like a party prop on his enormous head. "No, Bill," he said, "if I were in charge of the case, I'd have started with the very strong supposition that your wife was murdered."

5

"... Your wife was murdered ... if it were my case, I think I'd have a good deal to say to Mr. Caplin." Though Pode had left him Bill still seemed to hear the man's voice speaking to him across the table.

And whatever the police might think, there was something wrong. Mary was said to have blundered out in front of the lorry, John Caplin was a man with a record of dishonesty, and he himself couldn't even remember where he was at the time she died. Though they'd told him that his loss of memory had been caused by shock and the injury to his head, he was beginning to get the horrible feeling that it might somehow be connected with her death. He stared at the beer stains and cigarette burns on the table and tried to push through the barrier of his mind.

Sedale! A place called Sedale in the Peak District, where something had happened and almost a day had been erased from his life. But just what could it have been? He'd never been to the place before and he couldn't have met anybody he knew. He'd planned the whole trip like that; purposely avoiding anywhere where he might bump into a friend or acquaintance. All he wanted was to be alone—to finish the damned book and then get back to London.

He could remember much more about the book now. The original ending, for example, was quite clear to him. He'd driven the Dormobile to the end of a rough moorland track— that was where he'd broken the exhaust pipe, of course—and parked it beside a little stream. Apart from a few grazing sheep and the curlews sweeping backwards and forwards across the heather, he'd been quite alone there.

Then he'd started to write. Page 196 ... Chapter 12. In that version Roger hadn't gone to Paris at all. He'd called on the man he suspected of being Jane's lover and after a long, soul-searching conversation he'd known his suspicions were groundless.

Yes, that was correct. It must have still been morning when he'd read through the pages, tucked them away in the folder, and made himself a cup of coffee, knowing that by evening he should have knocked out the grand reconciliation scene to Max Mayer's full satisfaction.

It had happened while he had been drinking that coffee. He could see the picture quite clearly: the desk screwed to the side of the van, the typewriter, the green folder containing his manuscript beside it, and thin rain beating on the windows and running down in rivulets. And suddenly, almost as though he was being forced to do so, he had reached out and opened the folder and torn the last chapter to shreds. Then he had sat down beside the typewriter with the strong feeling that somebody was standing behind him, with arms reaching over his shoulders and fingers beating the keys.

And Pode had said that he thought Mary might have been murdered; pushed in front of the lorry or deliberately run down by it! But who was Pode? A silly old man who had retired long ago and gone senile? A tough, efficient cop who still knew his job? He had no way of telling that, but he was going to act on what Pode had implied. His wife was dead. He'd mourned for her, but he owed her more than that. If there was the slightest suspicion that her death was not an accident, it was up to him to find out exactly how she had died. He also had to know just what had happened at Sedale and blotted out his memory. Somehow he was quite sure that it was connected with her death, though he didn't know why. He looked up with a jerk as a hand touched his shoulder.

"You all right, sir?" A barman had come over to clear the table. "Not feeling ill or anything, are you?"

"No, I'm all right." Bill glanced at the clock; seven thirty already. He had sat there for over an hour since Pode had left, with his head bowed on the table and only a thimbleful of whisky in front of him. No wonder the man thought he was sick, or more likely tight.

"Yes, I'm quite all right, thank you; just a bit tired. Need some fresh air, perhaps." He stood up and tucked the type-script under his arm, seeing a dozen faces turn suspiciously towards him from the bar counter, feeling a dozen pairs of eyes bore into his back as he went out.

It was really dark now. Dark and cold and wet with the river mist thickening into halos around the street lamps and a thin moon swirling in cloud. He stood uncertainly on the pavement for a moment and then turned into the station and bought a ticket for West Norwood.

Briarhill Road looked as though it had seen better days a long time ago. It began outside West Norwood station and ran towards the slope up to the Crystal Palace where the lights on the television masts were flickering like a ship's distress signals through the drifting fog. Far above them Bill could hear the beat of a circling aeroplane.

He tightened his coat against the thin rain and walked for-ward. A parade of modern shops came first, a closed-down cinema, a church surrounded by tombstones that reminded him of rows of rotten teeth and at last tall Victorian houses standing back among dripping elms. Big, solid houses which looked as though they had been built by prosperous merchants a hundred years ago. Warm, comfortable houses, if you could afford to employ five indoor servants, with high gables and porches like four-poster bedsteads and plaster urns in front of the broad steps that ran up to them. The houses of rich men which had been designed to show that on their empire the sun would never set and a pound sterling would always be worth a golden sovereign.

It was easy enough for him to imagine what had happened. The rich men had died and their sons and grandsons had moved away; out of the suburbs or farther still to Surrey and Sussex, Haywards Heath and Dorking and Epsom and the green lawns of the stockbroker belt. Now the sun had not merely set, but performed a total eclipse over the empire, the pound was worth less than two dollars eighty cents, and the big, pretentious houses had had it. They had been cheaply converted and let out into rooms and flats and allowed to decay. Even in the mist and gloom Bill could see the ruin of the gardens, the crumbling timber that hadn't been painted for years, and the deep cracks and rifts in the stucco. The whole area had obviously been condemned and would soon be torn down to make way for council flats.

But for the moment some of them were still occupied. Lights blazed from several of the uncurtained windows, a record player blasted the latest pop tune across the street, and though it was dark and raining children were playing in the weed-ridden gardens.

No names and very few number plates on the gateposts, though. Bill paused uncertainly halfway up the hill and checked the address he had copied from the inquest report. "Ascayne House, Number 350." He turned into a drive towards three children, one white and two coloured, who were busily building a wigwam on what had once been a tennis court.

"Ascayne House, mister?" The two smaller children withdrew as he approached but the elder, who bore a strong resemblance to Dr. Hastings Banda, stood his ground defiantly. "Ain't no such place."

"Oh yes, there is." Bill took a shilling from his pocket and juggled it up and down in his hand. "It's somewhere near here. Number 350. Probably an old house divided into flats."

"Number 350?" The smallest child approached cautiously. "But that's just part of Rat Island now."

"Rat Island?" Bill's hand closed over the coin. He had no time for any make-believe games at the moment. "Just tell me where it is, my dear."

"But why do you want to know, mister?" Dr. Banda's eyes

were riveted on his closed fist. "There's nobody living there any more."

"Oh yes, there is. A man called John Caplin lives there. Now where is it?"

"John Caplin?" The third child stared up at him. "Did he used to drive a lorry? A big red lorry?"

"That's right, a big red lorry. Now where does he live?"

"It was on the top of the hill; a great tall house like a castle. But what Peter says is right, mister. There's nobody there any more. They all went away. It was unfit for human habitation—con—con . . ."

"You mean it was condemned? And did Mr. Caplin go too?"

"Everybody went." Even with the promise of reward the children were getting bored with his disbelief. "They went away two weeks ago. Now it's not a house any more; just part of Rat Island."

"I see. Thank you very much." Bill handed over the shilling and walked on. Just his luck! He had no clear idea of what he would say to John Caplin, but he knew he had to talk to him. It would probably be impossible to find out where the tenants had been moved to before morning.

Rat Island! Halfway up the slope the road curved round to form a crescent and it was easy to see how the area had got its name. There was not a light showing in any of the windows and most of the houses had been empty for a long time. Number 350 must have been the last to remain occupied.

"A great tall house like a castle." This was it all right. The place looked enormous in the gloom, and he could see mock towers and battlements rearing up above the roof and a huge square porch straight in front of him. It had obviously been designed for a man who was not only very rich, but had delusions of grandeur as well.

Bill pushed back the sagging gate. The drive was covered by a layer of fallen leaves and under them he could feel deep ruts which could have been made by Caplin's lorry. Mary had told him that Star Construction were considerate employers who often allowed drivers to take their vehicles home when public transport had stopped for the night. He stepped into the porch, hoping to find a card giving the tenants' change of addresses, but there was nothing there at all. The door was open, though, swinging backwards and forwards on rusty hinges with the glass panels broken and the mortice lock torn away from the woodwork. Wondering what penalties there might be for entering a condemned and deserted building, he pushed through it, flicking on his cigarette lighter and turning the flame up to peak.

He was in a big dark hall that had once been panelled in oak, but the panels had been stripped to show damp plaster and rotting brickwork, with here and there a run of battens which had supported it. The banisters of the staircase were broken and twisted and at the foot of the stairs a wooden plaque hung crazily from a single screw—"First Floor, Flats 2 & 4 . . . 2nd, 5 & 6 . . . 3rd, 7, 8 & 9."

Holding the lighter in front of him and hoping that the gas would last, Bill moved up the stairs. He was not normally afraid of the dark, but this house would be a maze of corridors and the stench of dry rot told him that at any moment a board might give way under his feet.

First floor! The landing felt loose and sagging and he could imagine the grey fungoid jackets wrapped around the joists that held it. His feet crunched on a heap of fallen plaster and in the lighter flame he could see a line of slogans chalked and carved on to the walls. "Peace and Socialism"—"Kick the Blacks Out"—"Bertie Allen Stinks." At the top of the next staircase a bedroom door was open showing an iron bedstead, a chest of drawers lying on its side, a cracked bentwood chair; all the useless lumber which it had not been worth the trouble of removing.

Second floor. Here the boards felt even more spongy and a gust of foul air blew down the corridor towards him and merged with the stink of rot. The house seemed not merely decayed, but evil too, filled with despair and the stench of fifty years of neglect. At the end of the landing pinpoints of eyes were watching him and he could hear a scurry of tiny feet. "Not a house any more, mister—Rat Island." It was only two weeks since the tenants moved out, but already other occupants had taken over.

Flat 8. Flat 9. Caplin's flat. The door had been torn from its hinges and left lying on the landing, and through a dusty window the glow of a street lamp showed up the little hall-cum-sitting room. As in the flat below he could see the litter of abandoned articles of furniture: a table with one of the legs missing, a length of mouldering carpet and a cupboard that had spilled a heap of papers on to the floor. He knelt down beside the papers hoping that one of them might tell him where Caplin had gone.

A football-pool coupon, the final gas bill, a calendar showing an oversized girl in tights squatting on top of a beer bottle, a letter—"Dear Sir, As we have written to you on three occasions regarding payment of the above account—." A betting slip made out for a horse named Flyaway George that had run and lost at Epsom, another letter demanding money. Caplin obviously did not believe in paying his bills promptly. At least he knew that much about him. Another betting slip, two more bills, a post-office savings book that showed no credit, a crumpled newspaper. There was nothing to be learnt there. Bill started to get to his feet and, as he did so, he stiffened. Just to his right there was the door of another room and it had started to swing open in the breeze. Through it he could see that he was not alone.

Very cautiously Bill moved towards the door and raised his lighter. The man half sat, half lay back in a cane chair with his feet stretched straight out in front of him. He was dressed in a leather jacket and a pair of corduroy trousers and there was a signet ring on his right hand that glinted in the flame. He was a very big man, but his face and hands looked as thin and white as a skeleton's, and the grey muffler that was wrapped around his throat stirred slightly in the current of stale air. There was a bottle by his side with a pile of cigarette stubs around it. John Caplin must have come back to collect some belongings and decided to have a last celebration in the old homestead. In the far corner of the room something scurried, something screamed. Rat Island!

"Mr. Caplin," he said. "I'm very sorry to disturb you, but—" The lighter showed up the details of the thin hands and Bill's whole body grew rigid, for they almost did belong to a skeleton. The bones stood out sharp and hard against the corduroy, though there were still shreds of skin and tissue hanging from them like chewed string. At the same instant the grey muffler twisted, turned to show a flash of eyes and teeth, and dropped to the floor so that he could see the long gash that it had torn in the man's throat. John Caplin was dead—he had died a long time ago and the new occupants of the house had started to pick him clean.

6

"The Inspector shouldn't be long, sir." The duty sergeant glanced at his watch. "Could I get you another cup of tea, Mr. Irwin? They say that it's good for the nerves."

"No, no thank you, Sergeant. My nerves are much better now." Bill shook his head and stubbed out another cigarette into the ash tray; the tenth he had smoked since coming into the room. Already his experiences seemed days ago, or almost as though they had happened to somebody else. The horror of seeing the rat twist away from the torn throat, the lighter flickering over the fleshless hands, and the shambling, stumbling run down the stairs and out to a phone booth. With its smell of polished wood and linoleum, the sporting trophies in the glass case and pictures of large men holding footballs and cricket bats, the police-station waiting room was like part of another cleaner world.

"Ah, here he is now, sir." The sergeant stood up as footsteps sounded in the corridor and the door opened. "Mr. Irwin, Inspector."

"Thank you, Wilson. I won't need you for a few minutes." The uniformed inspector watched the door close behind him and beamed on Bill. He was a plump, comfortable-looking man, with a face which could have belonged to a friendly bank manager who hates to refuse a valued customer; an insurance agent whose only concern is the client's welfare.

"Good evening to you, Mr. Irwin," he said. "My name's Macbeth, but don't—please don't reply 'The devil himself could not pronounce a title more hateful to mine ear.' I get that at least once a month and it's becoming a little tiresome."

"Of course I won't, Inspector." Bill stood up and smiled as was obviously expected of him; the worried client in the banker's office being put at his ease.

"Thank you. But do sit down again, Mr. Irwin." Macbeth waved him back to his chair and pulled up another for himself.

"Yes, you've had a very nasty experience, haven't you? Brrr, rats! Horrible creatures! Never could stand them myself. The sooner they get that Briarhill Road area cleaned up the better. Now I'll be as quick as I can and then a squad car can run you home." He laid a sheet of typescript on the table and frowned at it.

"Well, Mr. Irwin, I've read through the statement you made to Sergeant Wilson, and it's very clear. At around about eight o'clock this evening you went to that house on Briarhill, looking for John Caplin. You found him under most unpleasant circumstances and then ran out and phoned us. The reason you wanted to see Caplin was that he was the driver of a lorry which knocked down and killed your wife. By the way, I was very sorry to hear about that. A cigarette, sir?" He held out his packet.

"Now, Mr. Irwin, there's just one thing that I'd like you to clear up for me. What exactly did you want to say to Caplin?"

"What did I want to say to him?" Bill struggled to concentrate. "I don't honestly know, Inspector. I wanted to ask him

about the circumstances of my wife's death. It has been suggested to me that it might not have been an accident. Earlier
this evening I met a man ..." The smoke of their cigarettes
seemed to thicken into a mist and through it he saw Pode's
heavy, sagging face and heard his old pompous voice droning
on and on against the background murmur of the saloon bar.

"You probably know him, Inspector. His name is Pode; an
ex-superintendent of police. He said that my wife might quite
possibly have been murdered."

"Pode!" Macbeth's smile was replaced by a frown of annoyance. "George Pode, eh! I think you'd better tell me exactly
what he said to you, Mr. Irwin." He sat quite still listening
to Bill's story, and then got up and paced across the room in
thought.

"I see. Thank you, sir. Yes, I can quite understand why you
should have gone round to see Caplin after hearing that."
Macbeth paused and stared up at one of the groups of cricket-
ers on the wall.

"People grow old, Mr. Irwin," he said at last. "They grow
old and sometimes they become very bitter when they feel
they have been passed over. I've known Georgie Pode since I
was a young cop on the beat, and I'm afraid that that happened
in his case. He was very upset when he had to retire, though
for a time those newspaper articles gave him a lot of pleasure.
Then they came to an end as well, and he became a very sad
man indeed. He tries to hire himself out as a private inquiry
agent these days, but I shouldn't think he does much business.
Police methods have changed a lot since his heyday. Poor old
Georgie! Just a has-been now." The inspector returned to his
chair and glanced at the typescript again.

"But he didn't seem like that at all." Once again the loud,
self-confident voice rang through Bill's thoughts.

"I'm sure he didn't, Mr. Irwin, but I'm telling you the truth.
As he said, George Pode has a hobby. I don't suppose that
there's a case of violent death reported in the newspapers
which he doesn't read up and give the most sinister interpre-

tations to. Meeting you by chance in that pub would seem like a gift to him. I suppose he said that the police had mishandled the case." He grinned at Bill's nod.

"Yes, I'm sure he did. The police are fools, the Felcliff coroner is a fool, and who is the only wise man? Georgie Pode, the Scourge of the Criminal. As a literary man you'll remember your *Wind in the Willows,* Mr. Irwin. There's a couple of lines that apply to him, I think. 'The learned men at Oxford know all that there is to be knowed, but not one of them knows a tenth as much as intelligent Mr. Toad.'" Macbeth stubbed out his cigarette and leaned back in the chair.

"Yes, the police say that your wife's death was a simple accident, but who knows better? Georgie Pode, and if you employ his services he will run down her killer for you."

"But it wasn't like that." Bill shook his head, remembering just what Pode had said to him. "He didn't offer to help. He didn't even give me his card."

"He will do, Mr. Irwin, don't you worry. I'd bet a month's salary that before the week's out old George will approach you again.

"But we're not all fools, you know, and we have the facts of the case. I've been on the phone to the Felcliff police and also to Inspector Carne whom you've met. They are quite sure your wife was killed accidentally, and I can see no reason to connect her death with Caplin's murder."

"Then he was murdered?"

"Yes, he was murdered all right. There was a four-inch knife wound in his back. As far as the doctor can tell without a post mortem he's been dead for about a week. Won't you have another cup of tea, though? Sure?" Tea seemed to be the highlight of police hospitality and Macbeth looked slightly put out by Bill's refusal.

"As it happens, we know quite a lot about Mr. Caplin and he was a pretty bad boy; take your eyes and call back for the sockets if you gave him half a chance. He was in need of money, too; chaps dunning him all the time, though that can happen to the best of us. It seems that apart from having to keep his wife and two kids in that dump on Briarhill, there was another establishment containing a twenty-year-old blonde in Camden Town. He drank heavily and he gambled most unsuccessfully. He needed a lot more money than Star Construction paid him as a driver, in fact."

"Yes, I know that." Bill could still see those crumpled letters on the floor: "Dear Sir . . . Unless . . ." "But why was he murdered?"

"Well, we can't be sure of that at this stage, Mr. Irwin, but I have my theories. For some time past we've suspected that Caplin was the contact man for a gang of lorry thieves. He was on a regular run between Star's London depot and Felcliff, and he would have talked to a lot of other drivers in transport cafés and so on. By all accounts he was a pleasant chap to talk to and they might have confided in him. 'What are you carrying tomorrow, Jack?' 'So many cartons of cigarettes, eh!' 'And you, Sam?' 'So many crates of whisky!' Very useful information for a gang."

"But why should they murder him?"

"Thieves fall out, Mr. Irwin, and whatever the saying, there's very little honour amongst them. Perhaps friend Caplin got greedy and wanted a bigger cut. Perhaps he tried to blackmail somebody who turned nasty. Sound feasible to you?"

"I suppose so." Bill nodded, but he didn't really agree at all. John Caplin had driven a lorry which had killed his wife and a week later he had been murdered. There was just too much coincidence about it.

"But what do you think he was doing in that house, and why wasn't he reported missing days ago? You said he'd been dead for about a week."

"Easy questions, sir." Macbeth leaned forward and smiled. The kindly bank manager straightening out his customer's affairs. "Firstly, what better place could there be for a confidential meeting than a deserted house? Secondly, who would miss him? After the accident he told Star's transport manager that his nerves were badly shot up and they granted him leave of absence. His wife and kids had been moved out with the other tenants and she thought he was with his floosie at Camden Town. That lady on the other hand thought he was safe with his family in a council hostel. If you hadn't gone looking for him, the chances are that his body, or what was left of it, would have remained unnoticed till the demolition workers moved in."

"Or what was left of it!" Bill closed his mind against the picture of that grey shape writhing on Caplin's neck.

"Quite so, sir, but it doesn't do to dwell on these things." Macbeth lifted his house telephone. "Send a car round to the front for Mr. Irwin please, Sergeant." He pushed back his chair and stood up.

"And now, sir, I think we should start you on your way home. You've had a very nasty shock indeed, and I understand that you've been ill. I don't need to bother you any more." His handshake was dry and firm and full of good humour.

"You'll see the report that we've arrested Caplin's killers before long, and take my word for it that Georgie Pode is just an unbalanced old troublemaker who is talking nonsense. Your wife wasn't murdered, Mr. Irwin. She was killed in an accident."

7

There was no motive at all and everybody said that Mary had been killed accidentally. Everybody except Pode, that is, and according to Inspector Macbeth, Pode was an interfering eccentric, if not an actual lunatic. All the same, Bill was not completely convinced that Pode was wrong. John Caplin might have been killed by a gang of lorry thieves, but there was a lot of coincidence about it.

It was a lovely day. The final surge of summer probably, with sunlight dappling on the gold and scarlet leaves and morning mist still rising from the grass. From the Hyde Park Corner underpass he could hear a constant hum of traffic and scarlet buses lurched and swayed towards Marble Arch. The kind of day when it would be nice to get into a car and drive off without aim or purpose—to drive anywhere. Like hell it would be! He'd done that before and what had he come home to?

Monk's Close was a four-storeyed block of flats that had been built shortly before the war. From the outside it appeared unimpressive, almost dowdy in comparison to the new office blocks that surrounded it, but only on the outside. As soon as he stepped through the doorway, Bill could smell money: a great deal of money. The hall was white marble, marble statues stood in alcoves around the walls and a fountain played over a fish pond in the centre of the floor. The lift gates could have been guarding an Egyptian tomb, and the lighting was concealed behind Wedgwood plaques that seemed to be genuine. The atmosphere was about as cheerful as a museum, and to get a tenancy there would not only take money but a lot of influence as well.

"Can I help you, sir?" A very beautiful man in a dove-grey uniform that was even more beautiful bowed from behind a desk that appeared to have been carved out of a block of jade. He looked as though he didn't think much of Bill's suit and was trying not to show his feelings.

"Sir Norman Star's apartment?" He smiled briefly, but his tone gave no indication whether Star lived there or not. "Could I have your name? Thank you. Mr. William Irwin to see Mrs. Wayne. If you would excuse me for a moment." As he picked up the telephone Bill caught a slight whiff of Chanel Number 5. He also noticed that there was no staircase in the hall and no list of flat numbers. The inhabitants of Monk's Close obviously valued their privacy and were screened from the world like Arabian Nights princesses.

"Thank you—thank you very much. I'll bring Mr. Irwin up directly." The man replaced the telephone and smiled across the desk. His smile was quite different—a wide beam of welcome—and he seemed to approve of Bill's suit now.

"I'm very sorry to have kept you waiting, Mr. Irwin, but I'm sure you understand. We have to be very, very careful." The slight wave of his hand indicated legions of unwelcome callers: newspaper reporters, spongers, collectors for charity.

"Now, if you'd be kind enough to come with me, sir, I'll take you up to Sir Norman's apartment." He moved gracefully round from behind the desk and Bill saw that there was one flaw in the hang of his uniform: it bulged a little under the left armpit. He chalked up copy for future reference as he followed him to the lift, past the statues, the Wedgwood plaques and the fountain playing over the fish pool. Though it might be necessary for very rich people to protect their privacy, he hadn't realized that any London hall porters carried guns.

"Kom in plis, Mr. Ervine." A little dark maid whose voice he recognized from the telephone opened Star's door and left him in a big sunlit room with a deep curtsy and instructions to, "Vate—vate—plis vate."

Bill waited. He waited a long time, but it didn't seem like that, for the room interested him at once. By all accounts Star was a very tough citizen indeed; a self-made man who had fought his way to the top by a mixture of luck, brilliance and complete ruthlessness; a rough diamond with the accent on rough rather than the stone. This room belonged to somebody who had not only money but taste to go with it.

Yes, great taste where individual pieces were concerned, but the general effect of the room was quite wrong. He stared up at a Dürer engraving clashing slightly with a Francis Bacon painting, the Spode plates above the fireplace jarring against the Dresden figures on the mantelshelf and a case of Georgian silver glinting in the sunlight. Beside it was an open tray littered with porcelain snuffboxes, Egyptian scarabs and jade figurines. He ran his finger over one, feeling the coldness of a long-dead civilization taking the warmth from his skin, and then turned as footsteps sounded in the hall.

"You like my little collection, Mr. Irwin?" Sir Norman Star stood in the doorway and he was huge; a great craggy man with a body that looked as though it had been roughly carved out of oak straining against his dark business suit, and a face that might have been beaten by hammers into the scarred, battered shape it was. As he looked at him Bill suddenly realized the meaning of a biblical phrase he had never fully understood. A blind man who had often felt the roughness of bark could easily have exclaimed, "I see men as trees walking," if the first man he had seen had looked like Norman Star.

"Yes, I have some nice pieces, I think, but the general effect is terrible." Star grinned as he came forward into the room and exactly echoed Bill's thoughts. "I collect willy-nilly, I'm afraid, like an educated magpie with a little taste, but no broad vision.

"But let me introduce myself. My name is Star—Norman Star."

"Yes, I know that, Sir Norman." There was a deep humility in the introduction, coming as it did from a man whose picture appeared regularly in the financial pages of the newspapers. "I'm afraid your maid may have made a mistake and put me into the wrong room. I came to see your stepdaughter, Mrs. Wayne."

"No, no, Mr. Irwin, Anna made no mistake, and Ruth will be along in a few minutes. The fact is that I rather wanted to have a word with you first. But please sit down." He waved Bill to the sofa and lowered himself on to a frail Regency chair which looked as though it would split apart under his weight.

"Can I offer you anything by the way? A cup of coffee? A drink, perhaps? Yes, it is rather early for me as well." Star nodded at Bill's refusal. His voice was a complete medley of accents and he might have been born of American parents, looked after by an English nannie and educated in Europe.

"Now, Mr. Irwin, may I first say how very sorry I was to hear of the death of your wife. Let me see—how long had she been with us? Yes, over three years, and in the circumstances . . ." Once again Bill winced at the words "though an accident"—"without prejudice"—"compensation."

"No, Sir Norman," he said. "Your son-in-law, Allan Wayne, wrote to me along those lines. I haven't replied yet, but when I do, I shall tell him that I don't want any compensation."

"Will you indeed, Mr. Irwin—will you really?" Star grinned again and his right hand beat a slow tattoo on the arm of his chair. "You don't look like a fool, but in my experience only fools or rogues refuse money. No, your wife was at Felcliff on my firm's business, and whether you like it or not we will pay you compensation. What you do with the money, of course, is your own affair. Give it to charity if you like. By the way, I am also sorry to hear what happened last night. It must have been a very unpleasant experience."

"You know that—about Caplin?" Bill started slightly.

"Yes, I know about it. The police told my transport manager that he had been killed and also that he may have been connected with a gang stealing from lorries. It seems they want to make a sort of security check on some of our other drivers.

"But I didn't ask you here to discuss Caplin, Mr. Irwin. What I want to talk about is your wife and the circumstances of her death."

"My wife? You mean that you don't think that it was an accident?"

"I didn't say that, Mr. Irwin. In my own mind I am quite convinced that her death is best described as an accident. All the same I am very interested in your wife's movements during the last few days of her life." Star got up from his chair and crossed to the window, staring out across the park with the sunlight shining on his battered face and showing up the beads of scar tissue on the forehead and right cheek. The face of a man who had suffered deeply and was still suffering. As Bill watched him, he could see that for all his wealth Star was still an exile, a lonely old man who could never really belong to anything because there was too much mixture in him. Jew in the curved fleshy nose, the flaunting nostrils, and the full lips beneath them. Slav in the high cheekbones and—? Yes, only a Prussian could have produced that odd pear-shaped head that seemed to run straight back into the shoulders almost without the dignity of a neck. Star's face was like pieces of a jigsaw puzzle that didn't match and had been squeezed together by brute force.

Star? Stern? He struggled to remember what he knew about the man's background. Yes, Morgenstern—Emmanuel Morgenstern—in '39 a small builders' merchant in Lemberg. In '45 one tiny part of the rubble of Europe; a grey skeleton in a striped uniform trying to cheer as the first Allied troops entered the camp, trying to wave to them, trying to smile even and probably failing on every count.

But then the cards had changed and Emmanuel Morgenstern had come back to life. Lazarus had been raised, but not by any miracle. Unlike Jumbo Wayne he hadn't merely married the boss's stepdaughter; he'd married the boss herself. Margaret Bain, widow of a civil engineering contractor on Tyneside, who busied herself with good works on behalf of the refugees, had noticed him, taken a fancy to him, and within six months they were married. The D.P.'s card changed to a British passport, his name was anglicized, and the firm of Bain and MacIntyre became Star Construction. When his wife died of a heart condition three years later, leaving him with a stepdaughter of sixteen and twenty thousand pounds' capital apart from the business, he was already on the way up. Within another year he turned the firm into a public company, the City of London saw that they were on to a good thing, and the scarlet star and crane device started to blaze on every horizon.

"Yes, Mr. Irwin," he said, turning from the window at last and smiling at Bill. "I am very interested in your wife's movements during the week before her death, though I still think that was a sort of accident. The attack on you when you returned home was no accident, however."

"You know about that? You believe that it really happened?" Bill almost stammered out the words.

"Yes, I know about it, Mr. Irwin. I am also quite convinced that it happened just as you said. But may I give you a cigarette? They are supposed to steady the nerves and yours seem to be in a bad way." He took a case from his pocket and held it out to Bill.

"By and large the police in this country are hard-working and intelligent men, Mr. Irwin, but they have a weakness; they go only on facts. They have to, of course, or we might get cases of considerable injustice, but sometimes it is a hindrance to them, I imagine. In your case the facts were quite clear. They found no signs of breaking and entering in your flat, nothing of value seemed to be missing, and there was your blood on the bedroom scales, as though you had fallen and cut your head on them. The only suggestion of a burglar came from you yourself and you had been subjected to considerable mental shock. Can you blame them for doubting your story?"

"No, I don't blame anybody, Sir Norman." Bill leaned forward towards Star's lighter. "But you—you said that you believed my story. Why?"

"Because I have more facts than the police. You see, apart from reading the newspaper accounts, I think I know what your—the word burglar hardly applies in this case—what your mysterious visitor could have come for." He pushed the lighter back into his pocket and sat down. Once again the frail little chair looked as though it might shatter under his bulk. "Mr. Irwin, have you heard of my construction engineer, Hans Witzleb?"

"Yes, of course I have." The question must have been purely rhetorical, for who had not heard of Witzleb? Three years ago the name had made the headlines of every national paper. "Key Job for Nazi Boss." "Should this man be allowed to work here?"

Yes, Witzleb had made his mark all right. Technical assistant to Obersturmbannführer Willi Frenzel who had a list of murders like a telephone directory to his name; Planning Engineer to "Organization K," Frenzel's brain child, which controlled all civil engineering works in Germany and her occupied countries from '43 to '45 and employed over a million slave labourers. Witzleb had stood trial for crimes against humanity at the end of the war, but there was no evidence that he had been anything but a technician and he had only served two years' imprisonment on a minor charge. There matters should have rested and Witzleb allowed to rot in obscurity, but Norman Star had had other ideas. Three years ago he had contacted Witzleb and offered him a key post with Star Construction. The commotion which followed had filled the papers for a week. Petitions, protest marches, a vote of no confidence in Parliament and a token strike in the building industry, but Star had got his way. Willi Frenzel, the evil genius of "Organization K," was dead. He had died horribly, burned by jellied phosphorus during an R.A.F attack on Hamburg, but his minion was alive and kicking; chief engineer of Star Construction, with a British work permit and a salary which was rumoured to be well over twenty thousand pounds a year.

"Yes, of course I've heard of Witzleb," Bill said, "but what has he got to do with the man who attacked me in the flat?"

"Everything, Mr. Irwin, or almost everything." Star smiled slightly. "But will you tell me something? Were you among the people who thought I was wrong to employ him?"

"Yes, I was. As it happens I signed a petition."

"I see. Yes, I thought you might have done." Star nodded and pulled gently on his cigarette. "You must be a hard man, my friend, to carry on hatred for so long. I myself am partly Jewish and I have suffered very badly from people like Witzleb's masters. One of them gave me this face, for instance. He used a length of barbed wire wrapped round a stick." He rubbed his hand across the scar tissue on his cheek and forehead.

"All the same, I believe that people change with time, Mr. Irwin, and their beliefs and character often alter. I think we must give them the benefit of that doubt at least, if we are to call ourselves civilized. Hans Witzleb may have been a monster twenty years ago, but I don't think he is now. I think he is just a little man—an Unteroffizier—who likes to obey orders. As long as the orders are clear and definite it doesn't matter very much to him whether the person who gives them is named Frenzel or Hitler or Morgenstern. He is also one of the best civil engineers alive, and as a businessman I felt I should employ him. I have no cause to regret it either. Since he joined the firm our activities have increased by fifteen per cent and our overheads fallen by ten. My decision has paid off very well, in fact, and it would have paid still better if your wife hadn't done something very foolish."

"My wife!" Bill frowned at him. "Sir Norman, may we get down to facts? You used the expressions 'a sort of accident,' 'is best described as an accident,' when you mentioned her death. You also imply that you know more about the burglary than the police do. Will you please tell me exactly what you do know and what my wife had to do with Hans Witzleb?"

"In a moment—in just a moment." Star leaned forward and stubbed out his cigarette.

"I'll tell you everything I know, Mr. Irwin, but first I want to ask you one more question. Have you any idea how many tons of reinforced concrete would go into a building the size of this block of flats?"

He couldn't really understand the technical details, of course; hardening constituents and setting agents; tricalcium silicate and dicalcium aluminate; minute quantities of iron and soda and magnesium merging together to produce a rock-like substance which was also fragile; but the gist of it was clear enough. Hans Witzleb had been experimenting with an entirely novel form of cement; a substance that would produce concrete which would require hardly any reinforcement because it was not only as hard as rock, but as flexible as steel. A product that could cut the cost of a large building operation by as much as a third.

And he had succeeded; that was the point. After years of trial and error the proportions had come out right and once his final figures were copytyped he was going to have the process patented.

"And Mary had those papers?"

"That's right, Mr. Irwin. To the best of our knowledge your wife was the last person to have them. The whole thing was a bad departmental mix-up, if nothing worse." Star leaned back in the chair with the sunlight showing weariness as well as the scars on his face.

"What happened was this. Witzleb's own secretary was away from the office with influenza and he didn't like to entrust the papers to a girl from the pool. Your wife was in London for a couple of days on some business connected with the demolition program at Felcliff and he asked her if she would type them out for him. She promised to do them at home and send them round to the Patent Office as soon as she had finished."

"I see." Bill nodded. Mary had told him that she might be coming back to London for the odd night while he was away. "And did she know what those papers were?"

"I'm afraid I can't tell you that, Mr. Irwin. She knew they were important and I presume she would have known what the subject was, but I doubt if she would have understood the technical jargon. In any case she never finished them. The next morning my son-in-law, Allan Wayne, phoned her and told her to return to Felcliff immediately. He said he was having trouble with some plans, though that was not the real reason, as I will tell you later. Allan is a weak man, I'm afraid. He has always relied far too much on subordinates." There was more than the hint of a sneer in Star's voice. He looked as though he had never really relied on anybody in his life and couldn't forgive it in others.

"But the point is this. Your wife left those papers in her flat. She told Witzleb that when she saw him later in Felcliff. He was naturally worried, but she said they were in a perfectly safe place and that she would finish the typing as soon as she returned to London."

"But she never did return." In his mind's eye Bill could see the damp midnight streets, the loom of the telephone booth at the junction and hear the rumble of the approaching lorry. "And you think that the burglar who came in to the flat and laid me out might have been looking for those papers, Sir Norman?"

"I don't merely think so. I'm quite sure he was looking for them. Though Witzleb retained a copy of his notes, the originals would obviously be of enormous value to any of our rivals; more value than you could even begin to visualize." Star got up and pulled open the drawer of a little Sheraton writing desk by the door.

"And one of our rivals is an unscrupulous man, Mr. Irwin. I believe that he employed somebody to enter the flat and steal those papers. He was very well informed about everything and probably saw no danger in it. He knew that you were away from home and that your wife would be returning from Felcliff on the midnight train and could not get back to the flat before four o'clock in the morning. He thought he was quite safe, in fact." He had found what he wanted in the desk now. A single sheet of paper which he handed to Bill.

"Here is a specimen of Hans Witzleb's handwriting. Somewhere in your flat there are three foolscap pages with notes in the same hand. That is why I wanted to see you, Mr. Irwin. You must know where your wife would have hidden them. I want you to find them and return them to us. If you do I will be your debtor for the rest of my life."

"A perfectly safe place!" Bill frowned, thinking of secret drawers and safes hidden away behind pictures, and a square of panelling that at the touch of a button would slide back to reveal treasure trove. He was quite sure that there was nothing like that in the flat.

"But the police have searched the place thoroughly already," he said. "If what you say is correct, the burglar must have found them."

"No, he didn't get them. I'm quite certain about that. We have our spies too, and if my rival had got his hands on them I'd have heard about it by now."

"But why didn't you tell the police this?" Bill felt a sudden surge of anger as he looked at the cramped writing. It appeared to contain Witzleb's comments on the new dock installations at Felcliff. "They almost laughed when I told them about the burglar—they seemed to think I was mad."

"I know that, Mr. Irwin, and I am extremely sorry for the embarrassment it must have caused you. All the same I can't go to the police yet and I'm going to ask you to respect my confidence a little further. You see, though I'm quite certain that my rival went after those papers, I only have a suspicion as to who tipped him off about them. Believe me I hope—really hope that my suspicions are groundless." Star pressed a bell by his side and a moment later the maid appeared.

"Anna," he said, and his voice was very gentle. "Would you be kind enough to ask Mrs. Wayne to come here in five minutes' time, please? Thank you." He waited till the door closed behind her and then turned to Bill again.

"This is what I think may have happened, Mr. Irwin, but I don't want to act upon it till I'm quite sure." He pulled a watch out of his pocket and glanced at it. "Your wife returned to Felcliff, leaving Witzleb's papers somewhere in the flat. Who do you think she might have mentioned them to? Who would have known that she was not going back to London by the afternoon train on the next day, but on the night train which would not get her home before four o'clock in the morning? Who could have stolen her key? Who could have heard that you would be away for at least another couple of days?"

"I don't . . ." Bill started to shake his head but, even as he opened his mouth, he did know. There was only one person who answered the description. A jolly person who was always to be found in the noisiest circle of the cocktail party. A fat but agile person bounding and whooping across the tennis court and usually taking defeat with far better grace than victory. A person with a heavy face that always seemed to be in need of a shave, a heavy hand that pumped his own up and down, and a hearty voice roaring in his ear. "We're lucky chaps you and I, Billy boy. You've got the best little wife in the world and I have the best secretary." Jolly old Jumbo Wayne.

"Yes, you know all right, Mr. Irwin. Allan Wayne." Star's voice answered the question for him. "When things go his way, my son-in-law is a very estimable person and I have no complaints about him. I am quite certain that he married Ruth for love and I promoted him from a clerk in the drawing office to a top-level executive. I didn't make him a director, though. I didn't feel that Jumbo's abilities quite justified that.

"And at the beginning I think he was happy enough. He'd never dreamed of earning so much money, and Ruth was a very beautiful girl. Then she had that hunting accident, lust could no longer be gratified, and love went out of the window, as the saying goes." Star still smiled, his voice was still low and gentle, but Bill could see the sudden hardness in his eyes.

"Yes, poor Jumbo. No love, no directorship and no chance of a divorce without the certain loss of his job. I can't really blame him for trying to sell me out to a rival."

"I don't believe you, Sir Norman. I'm sorry, but I just can't believe you." Bill stared at the pattern on the carpet and struggled to concentrate. Nothing made sense—nothing tied up. Mary had been killed by a lorry and its driver had been murdered. He had lost part of his memory at a place called Sedale and Jumbo Wayne, a man he had always considered to be an amiable idiot, had organized a burglary at his flat. It was all quite crazy.

"I don't care whether you believe me or not, Mr. Irwin. All I want is your help in recovering those papers. For your own sake you have got to find them."

"Got to?" Bill started at the sudden guttural rasp in Star's voice.

"Yes, got to, young man. For two reasons. Remember that you were surprised by a thief who clubbed you on the head and then gave up the search. By now I imagine that his employers will probably think that you have the papers, Mr. Irwin, and are preparing to use them for your own ends. If that is the case it seems highly likely that they will kill you for them."

"And the second reason?" Bill could only stare foolishly at him.

"The second reason is purely revenge. Remember that Allan Wayne is going to profit very considerably if my rival gets hold of Witzleb's figures."

"Revenge. Because I was knocked out!" The word was ludicrous. Shades of Monte Cristo and Baroness Orczy—*I Will Repay.*

"No, don't smile at me, Mr. Irwin." Star hunched forward over the sofa scowling at him. "What I am going to tell you has nothing to do with what happened in your flat. Tell me something first, though. Were you and your wife happy together?"

Happy? Rows over money sometimes: "Darling, let's just buy it and blow the cost." Frequent disagreements about her job and occasional anxiety on his part that she might be drawing away from him, though he'd barely admitted that to himself. But on the whole . . . "Yes, Sir Norman," he said. "On the whole I think we were very happy."

"I see. Then I'm sorry, Mr. Irwin, but I may be going to hurt you a great deal. Will you excuse me for a moment, though?" There was a soft, scraping sound outside the door and Star got up and opened it.

When Bill had last seen her, Ruth Wayne had looked thin and ill, but now she looked as though she was dying. Apart from the dark lines under her eyes her face seemed almost transparent and her hands on the arms of the wheel chair were as thin as the hands he had seen in Caplin's rat-infested flat.

"This is my stepdaughter, Ruth Wayne." Star pushed her into the room towards him.

"Before your wife died, Ruth wrote you a letter asking you to call and see her, but after she heard about the accident she changed her mind. I was in the room when you phoned yesterday and I persuaded her that she must confirm what I have to say. You will do that, won't you, my dear?" The pale face nodded and he pulled on the brake of the chair. "Thank you.

"Mr. Irwin, the police are quite correct in saying that your wife was killed in an accident, but doesn't it seem strange to you why the accident happened—why a healthy, intelligent young woman should have stumbled out into the road as she did. I'm going to tell you why, Mr. Irwin, however much it hurts. Your wife walked in front of that lorry because she was in a state of shock. She had just been discarded."

"Discarded? You mean . . ." Bill stared at Star, but it was the girl in the wheel chair who answered him.

"Yes, discarded, Mr. Irwin. She was discarded because I said she must be." Rather horribly there seemed to be a slight glow of pride on her face. "You see I found out that your wife and my husband had been lovers for years."

8

Once, at Waterloo Underground station, Bill had seen a man killed by a train. He was an extremely drunk man and had obviously been to a very good party indeed. There were two friends with him and the three of them had shouted and occasionally burst into song, so that the other passengers gave them a wide berth. The man had slipped and fallen on to the platform with his legs dangling over the edge. He had laughed loudly when he found that he wasn't hurt and his friends had laughed with him. Then he stopped laughing as the train shot out of the tunnel and came towards him. Even with the noise of the train, Bill had heard him scream "No, no, no" just before it hit him, and he had never forgotten the look on his face. He had a feeling that his own face must have looked very similar as Ruth Wayne told him about Mary.

But it couldn't be true. They couldn't have been lovers. Not Mary—not Jumbo! Bill half-walked, half-staggered up the stairs to his flat and he gripped the rail, for he felt that at any moment his legs might give way under him.

No, not with Jumbo; he could have forgiven her anything except that. The huge, sweaty body whooping with triumph as his opponent's ball hit the tennis net, or shouting a war cry as it lumbered down the beach and plunged into the surf! The glistening face beaming at him through the smoke of a cocktail party and the boasts pouring out between the flow of dirty stories. "Having to use the old Bentley tonight, as the Lancia's in dock again. Mustn't grumble, though, and she's worth every penny of the four thousand quid I paid for her. Knocked up over a hundred and thirty down the M1 last month."

No, Mary couldn't have been his lover. The thought of her body against his matted chest and that loud, booming voice whispering endearments was not only repulsive but ludicrous.

But she had been—she damned well had been! Bill paused on the landing, remembering how Ruth Wayne had looked as she told her story. The suspicions of years hardening into certainty, a showdown, the denials and at last a promise.

Yes, Mary had been his mistress and Jumbo hadn't even loved her, that was possibly the most horrible thing of all. "Not to worry, old girl," he'd told Ruth. "You're wrong, of course, there was nothing between us, but I'll send her packing, if that's what you want. I wouldn't have thought it would have bothered you all that much, though, even if it were true. I mean, under the circumstances, since your accident, I'd have imagined you'd like me to have a bit of fun now and then."

But Ruth had objected to Jumbo's fun all right. As he'd listened to her, Bill had seen the will and determination in her sick white face. Though all normal relations were over between them, Jumbo was still a possession and she wasn't going to share her possessions with anybody else. He'd been given his ultimatum. He was to sack Mary, promise never to see her again or leave Star Construction with a testimonial which might—just might—get him a job as a clerk.

And like a good boy, Jumbo had given his promise without

even a tiny trumpet of defiance. He'd promised to do exactly what Ruth demanded and he'd done it at Felcliff. Probably it had seemed easier to him there. A nice quiet hotel room to talk things over in and no friends or relations she could run sobbing to.

"Damn him! Damn the bastard!" Bill muttered the words aloud as he groped for his key. Had she given Jumbo a key, he wondered? Somehow the very thought of entering the flat had become disgusting to him.

Yes, Jumbo had obeyed his orders all right. A telephone call from Felcliff had been the first move. "Mary, my darling . . ." Had he called her *darling?* "Please drop everything and come up here at once. Yes, something rather important has cropped up."

So the poor bitch had done just that—packed her bags and gone off ready for the chopper, leaving Witzleb's papers in the flat. Bill slid the key into the lock, feeling no anger against his wife, but deep revulsion against himself. He was the one who was really to blame for everything that happened. Jumbo and Mary must have seen each other's attractions when they'd first met on that Spanish holiday three years ago. It was there that Jumbo had suggested she might like to work with him. Only a Spanish word could describe himself: *cabrón*—a man who is unable to satisfy his woman.

The parting hadn't come as soon as she'd arrived back at Felcliff, of course. She'd spent the night there. A final night together, perhaps, before he told her about Ruth's ultimatum? And then in the morning she must have mentioned Witzleb's invention and Jumbo's mean little mind had started to click out a vision of security. Even after he'd broken off with Mary, Ruth might still decide to get rid of him and he had his future to think of. Just in case that happened a phone call to Star's corrupt business rival could guarantee him that future.

All that was merely what Star thought might have happened, of course, but he was inclined to back Star's judgment. He remembered a television interview with the man he had seen some years ago. The scarred face smiling into the camera and the strangely accented voice recounting his life and opinions. "Most of my financial success has been due to luck and the knack of assessing a situation very quickly. Apart from my building operations I control a timber firm in Scotland. Don't ask me why—I just can't tell you—but I am able to walk through a stretch of woodland and judge almost exactly how many cubic feet of sound timber it contains to the acre."

Yes, probably Star's suspicions were correct. Jumbo had contacted his rival and then made another phone call to Mary at her hotel. This time it would have been the call that mattered. "Finished—sacked—washed-up—done for—go to hell!" Jolly old Jumbo Wayne.

Damn him! Bill twisted the key in the lock and he could almost feel the thick neck between his hands as he considered the rest of it. The dark streets with the station clock jerking on towards midnight. Mary's feet stumbling down from the hotel with the loom of the phone box at the junction. She wouldn't have noticed the lights of the approaching lorry because she was weeping, and her ears wouldn't have heard the engine. All she could hear was Jumbo Wayne's voice repeating, "Finished." Then there would have been a scream, a sudden howl of air brakes, a curse from the driver, and a bundle of blood-stained rags rolling over and over in the gutter.

Yes, damn Jumbo! And damn Ruth Wayne if it came to that. Though he pitied her for her crippled body, he could still see that glow of pride in her face and there was something obscene in the thought of the sick woman denying life to the strong. Damn himself too! If he hadn't been so inadequate, so concerned with himself and his trashy scribbling, Mary would never have had that affair with Jumbo and still be alive.

He pushed open the door and stepped into the flat. As always there was the familiar smell of pinewood, hot pipes and lavender polish, but it seemed stronger than usual. Apparently Mrs. Carver had been on the job this morning. "Oh, Mr. Irwin, how the poor missus liked to see the place all nice and shiny when she came home. And even if she's not here to see it now, I'm going to make sure that it stays just that way."

Wood—pipes—lavender. And something else? A faint but pungent odour which didn't fit in with any of them. Smoke—tobacco smoke. The poor missus might have liked to see things all nice and shiny, but Molly Carver had obviously enjoyed a long coffee break. Good luck to her! Bill closed the door behind him and stood in the hall for a moment, considering Witzleb's notes and the possibility that Mary had hidden them in the flat. Though Star had seemed certain they were still there, he doubted it. There was no concealed safe, no secret drawer, no possible hiding place at all. He'd lived there for almost four years, hadn't he? He'd have been bound to have noticed anything like that.

The smell of smoke again! Thick, acrid smoke now, and it seemed to be getting stronger. He glanced at his watch. It was after one o'clock already and Mrs. Carver always left on the dot of twelve. No cigarette smoke could have hung about so long with the hall windows wide open and the curtains swinging in the breeze. Something was burning then and he could see where. The door of his office was partly ajar, and he could make out a curl of smoke drifting through it and spiralling up in the sunlight.

"... his employers will probably think that you have the papers, Mr. Irwin ..." Star's warning ran through his head and, almost as though it had a will of its own, he felt his body grow tense. "... I think it highly likely that they will kill you for them." He started to edge back towards the hall door, and then knew that that was no solution. His own life was no longer of any great value to him, and whoever had caused or was causing that smoke had to be faced. Just to the right of the door was a shelf with an ornamental brass Buddha resting on it. They had bought it last year, he remembered. Probably "Birmingham," but there was a certain serenity in the bland smiling face which he'd always liked. He picked it up, feeling the comfortable weight and hardness of the metal and also a slight sense of guilt; the symbol of peace about to be used as a weapon.

It was perhaps ten yards down the passage to his office, but it felt like a mile and at each step the floorboards seemed to creak and groan in warning. He paused by the doorway for a moment, hearing something move and somebody breathe in the room, then he raised the Buddha and kicked the door wide open. The drifting wisps of smoke thickened into a mist with the sunlight mottling through it to show the desk, the typewriter, the bookcase, the table, the man bent over the table. A big, paunchy man with a grey sagging face and a gun in his hand who swung round quickly as Bill rushed at him.

"Easy, old boy, just take it easy." An arm that was like a bolster case stuffed with bricks came flailing up to knock the Buddha out of Bill's grasp and a hand gripped his shoulder. "Yes, that's better."

"You—you ..." Bill could only stammer as the hand released him. "I thought you were ..."

"You thought I was another burglar, I suppose." Pode scowled down at the statuette on the carpet. "Shouldn't jump to conclusions, you know. Shouldn't come rushing in like that before knowing what's going on. If I hadn't been too quick for you, you might have done me a very serious injury with that thing." He moved into the light of the window and the gun became a short blackened pipe.

"But what are you doing here? How did you get in?" Bill stared at him and rubbed his arm. For all his apparent flabbiness, Pode packed a heavy blow. He felt as though he had been beaten with a cricket bat.

"I came in in a perfectly normal manner. Your daily help opened the door for me. Intelligent woman that! Quite a fan of mine too. It seems that she's read every one of those articles I did for the *Chronicle*. She was quite delighted to meet me in the flesh and told me to make myself at home till you came back. I did so." Pode grinned at the whisky bottle and glasses on the table, and Bill saw that he had carried out Mrs. Carver's instructions to the letter.

"As to why I called, that's simple enough too. I thought we should have a further chat. But aren't you going to have a drink yourself, old man? You look as though you could use one—look rather like the raw end of a nerve, if it comes to that. I told Mrs. Carver to lay out a glass for when you got back from old Star."

"Very thoughtful of you." Bill helped himself to his own whisky. "You knew that I'd gone to Star's flat?"

"Oh yes, I know quite a lot about your movements, old boy. As it happens, I told you a bit of a tale yesterday; about my not being on the case. The truth is that a certain party has asked me to make a few inquiries for him. I heard that you were seeing your publisher yesterday and thought I should arrange to bump into you." Pode lowered himself back into his chair and started to refill his pipe. "Sorry to hear about your experience last night. My fault in a way. I might have known that you'd go round to see Caplin after I suggested murder to you. I never thought they'd knock the blighter off so quickly, though. Oh yes, I know all about that. As I said, Inspector Carne is an old friend and he keeps me informed."

"I see. Macbeth told Carne about my finding Caplin's body and he passed on the information to you."

"Macbeth!" A pinkish tinge crept into Pode's grey cheeks. "You saw him at Norwood, did you? Damned little whipper-snapper. Just before my retirement I caught him out in a really crass piece of inefficiency and nearly bust him." His thumb rammed tobacco into the bowl of the pipe as though he were gouging out one of Macbeth's eyes. "Did you tell him that you'd talked to me? Did he say anything—anything at all objectionable about me?"

"Yes, I'm afraid he did." As he told him, Bill realized that Jumbo Wayne had been badly misnamed. This Pode was the real elephant. A great, pompous, aggrieved elephant with his heavy, sagging face and the little pink eyes glowering angrily out through the folds of his flesh.

"I see. He said that, did he? That I was merely an interfering old has-been." Pode pulled out a purple silk handkerchief and blew his nose violently. "Well, he's going to be in for a few surprises and the Norwood superintendent, a very good friend of mine, will hear a number of home truths about Inspector Angus Macbeth.

"Still, I didn't come over here to discuss him." He tucked away his handkerchief and applied a match to the pipe. "What did Star and Ruth Wayne have to say to you, old boy?"

"No, Superintendent. I think we should start with your story first. Just who are you working for and what is your interest in the case?"

"I'll bet you'd like to know that, old boy, but I'm not telling; not for the present, that is. May I?" The pipe was drawing to Pode's full satisfaction now, with clouds of acrid smoke pouring across the room, and he reached out and helped himself to another glass of whisky.

"Thanks. Quite good stuff this. No, Bill, at this juncture, I'm not going to confide in you, but I think you had better tell me everything you possibly can. You see I came here in the hope that you might help me. I am now quite certain that you won't be able to, but I've discovered something about you and I think you may be in trouble. Very bad trouble indeed, and you've been in it since the day you went to Sedale."

Sedale! The room and Pode's face faded and the days slid backwards. It was raining; a fine but persistent rain. The Dormobile was parked by the side of a stream and the road wound gracefully away in the distance across a desolate peaty moor cut by limestone walls that shone like metal in the wet. There was not a house in sight, but curlews were swooping over the bracken and here and there he could see a huddle of grazing sheep. Sedale: a road just outside a place called Sedale and something had happened to him there. Something unspeakable which he just couldn't remember. He started to ask Pode how he even knew that he'd been there, but broke off. Everybody—Pode—Sir Norman Star—Inspector

Carne—they all appeared to know everything and he knew nothing at all.

"Very well," he said. "I'll tell you."

"I see. So that's what they told you. Interesting, old boy. Quite interesting." Pode stared at the notes he had taken of Bill's interview with Star and Ruth Wayne.

"Now, let's see what we have. What we can accept as true—what is possibly true—what is quite definitely false." He knocked out his pipe, blew down the stem, wiped the bowl carefully on the sleeve of his coat and tucked it away in his pocket.

"This story of your wife having an affair with Allan Wayne. Yes, I'm afraid that that is probably true enough. Though Wayne denied it to his wife, it seems very likely and I've got some evidence which I'll show you in a minute or two.

"This business about the burglar you said was in the flat and laid you out on the morning you came home. Yes, I've changed my mind on that score. I didn't know quite what to believe at first, but now I'm sure it happened just as you told the police.

"That Caplin was murdered by a gang of lorry thieves. Yes, maybe. He was murdered by somebody, and even that fool Macbeth wouldn't have made a mistake about his being mixed up with a gang. We'll just have to see if they make an arrest and get the charge to stick. Mark it *Possibly True* for the time being." He scribbled a note in his pad.

"Now, what do we make of Norman Star's story about the papers which your wife is supposed to have left here when she returned to Felcliff? Yes, I have good reason to believe that she had something of the kind which one of Star's rivals would have given his eye teeth to get hold of."

"That appeared to be the general idea." Bill spoke quite innocently, but Pode flushed with annoyance.

"Yes, I'm sure it did, but don't try to be flippant with me, old boy. Don't try anything. Believe me you're in very great danger, as I'll show you in a few minutes.

"Anyway, let's assume that your wife had some papers which were very important to Star and Witzleb. I shouldn't think that they had anything to do with the manufacture of cement, however. Witzleb is a construction engineer, not a scientist, and Star is a very cagey old fox indeed. If you found the papers they would be in some technical jargon quite incomprehensible to a layman, and you wouldn't understand them. No, I don't think friend Star has told you what they really are."

"He seemed to be telling the truth."

"I'm sure he did. I never said he was a poor liar, did I?" Pode's face suddenly contorted as a deep rumble sounded from his stomach and he stifled a belch.

"Excuse me, Bill. My wife is a fool of a woman, I'm afraid. Goes on foreign holidays every year and apes the cooking when she gets home. It was Yugoslavia last time. Great plates of beastly greasy muck that give me hell. Never could stand wop dishes.

"But let's get on. Star's story is that your wife had some papers which were vitally important to him and Witzleb. I think we can believe that much. Your wife goes to Felcliff and tells Allan Wayne about them. Like a good loyal son-in-law, Wayne promptly contacts a corrupt business rival of Star's and spills him the beans. Yes, that could be possible. From all I hear Wayne is in pretty dire financial straits."

"What?" Bill craned forward. "But I understood he is making at least fifteen thousand a year."

"Quite correct." Pode consulted a note in the back of his pocketbook. "His actual salary is sixteen thousand five hundred, but the old man has a thing about expense accounts and won't allow him one. After tax that would leave him about seven thousand spending money. A hell of a lot to you and me, but very little to a chap with a megalomania which needs a house in Knightsbridge, three cars, an ocean-going yacht and a mistress to bolster it up. Sorry, Bill! I shouldn't have said that—about the mistress."

"It doesn't matter and it's probably true." Bill turned away from him and stared through the window. Beyond the bend of the river, the gasholders towered like Martian cities and a tug was dragging three barges against the tide. Yes, it was probably true, he thought, but somehow he still couldn't completely believe it.

"Good! No offence meant and none taken, eh?" Pode beamed at him and swigged back the remains of his whisky. "Well, we can assume that your wife did have some important papers which she mentioned to Wayne. We'll also assume that Wayne could easily have informed Star's mysterious rival about them and that he might have sent somebody over here to try and get hold of them. Mark that *Possibly True*. The idea of Wayne stealing her key to the flat is just poppycock, of course. Any boy scout could open that lock of yours with a nail file." He heaved himself up from his chair and stared at the bookcase as though the titles might somehow tell him what he wanted to know.

"We've got seven facts then. Two of them almost certainly true, four of them possibly true, and one of them quite definitely false: Star's suggestion that the papers might still be here."

"You mean that you've been searching the flat before I came back." For a moment Bill had just one ambition in life: to plant his fist hard in the centre of Pode's sagging belly. Two things restrained him. In the first place he was beginning to feel he had to trust Pode. Secondly, he felt sure that before his fist got home Pode would deliver some low, crafty blow and knock him senseless.

"Yes, I had a look round." Pode obviously imagined that he had acted well within his rights. "A damn sight more thorough look than the local bobbies had, I should imagine. From what Star told you, the papers are supposed to consist of three sheets of foolscap with notes in Witzleb's rather distinctive handwriting. I would gamble my whole reputation that they are nowhere in this flat."

"Then the burglar must have found them that night and Star's rival already has them."

"He either found them, or the whole story is a fabrication on Star's part, or your wife didn't leave them here at all. Thanks, I will have a refill, please." Pode held out his glass to Bill. "But let's leave the question of Witzleb's papers for a moment and go back to your wife's death. And before we do that, let's talk about your movements for a moment."

"My movements?" An unpleasant image of childhood crossed Bill's mind. A study that smelled of chalk and leather bindings and tobacco smoke. A table covered with green baize, photographs of school groups on the walls and the headmaster standing with his back to the fireplace and a cane in his hand. "I have dealt with the other offenders, Irwin, who appear to be merely dupes. Now I come to you: the ringleader of this sorry affair."

"Yes, your movements, old boy. Everything that you did since leaving this place Sedale, in fact. Cheers!" Pode took a swig of whisky and his smile widened. There was something almost hypnotic in his little bright eyes twinkling out through the grey folds of flesh. "Oh yes, you told the doctors and the police that you can't remember anything, but I'm here to help you. To try and help you that is.

"By the way, have you got a road map handy? Yes, that A.A. book will do fine. Thanks." He laid it on the desk and flicked through the centre pages.

"Now, where are we? Yes, when you left for your trip you asked Mrs. Carver to forward your mail to the post offices at Chester, Keswick, Appleby and this place Sedale, which was to be your last port of call before returning to London." A stubby, nicotine-stained finger traced the route.

"Well, we can forget about the earlier part of the trip. All that concerns us is what happened at Sedale and what you did after you left there. We know that you collected two letters from the local post office and we know that you finished the revised ending of your novel there."

"You know that?" Bill frowned. "You've been to see Max Mayer?"

"Yes, I've had a chat with Mr. Mayer this morning. A very agreeable fellow indeed. With any luck he may commission me to write a book of reminiscences for him. We should do very well out of it too, but that's neither here nor there. The point is that Mr. Mayer told me that you always date the first page of a day's work. The first page of the final chapter was dated the tenth of the month and the parcel had been posted from Sedale. You appear to have written it at a hell of a rate and it was packed solid with typing errors. We also know that you left Sedale at about three o'clock in the afternoon and drove towards the main road from Sheffield to London. No, no, Bill, don't keep repeating, 'How do you know that?' I'm going to tell you." Pode raised a great flipper of a hand and cut him short.

"The people I'm working for pay me pretty generously and I've had a colleague in the north make some inquiries. A shepherd recognized your car just outside Sedale—a grey-and-white Dormobile with a cracked exhaust being driven very fast towards the M8. He remembered it because the noise from the exhaust scattered his sheep. I've always said that anger is one of the best aids to memory.

"Now, what I want to know is this. You left Sedale at about three p.m. and arrived back here at four o'clock in the morning. We know that is correct, because a tenant in the ground-floor flat heard you draw up outside and heard the church clock strike at the same time. What bothers me is why the journey took you so long. Over thirteen hours to travel a hundred and fifty miles, most of which is on a motorway with a minimum permitted speed of forty miles an hour!"

"I stopped. I stopped several times. I wanted to get drunk, you see. I don't normally drink a great deal, but on that day—for some reason which I can't remember . . ." Bill broke off, remembering the smoke and noise of saloon bars. Brass winking over counters, the smell of spilled beer, and the accents of the customers changing as he got farther south. The Bull at Raynford—the George and Dragon at Selwicke, and a big plushy place with a name he couldn't remember, though there had been cards advertising it laid out all along the tables and bar counter.

"Yes, I'm sure you stopped, Bill, but British licensing laws would only have allowed you to stop for drinks between five thirty and eleven." Pode's voice ground on like an old, rusty saw hacking its way through rotten timber. "Not long enough to account for the length of time you took for the journey."

"But I might have parked the car in a lay-by and fallen asleep. I might have done anything."

"Yes, you might have fallen asleep. You might have made a detour. You might have done anything, as you say. I wonder if the second suggestion is the accurate one? Did you make a detour, perhaps—to Felcliff?"

"No, no, why should I?" Bill's mouth was suddenly dry and he could feel his heartbeats begin to speed up. "Felcliff would have been miles out of my way. Besides, I didn't think that Mary would be there. I thought that she would . . ."

"Quite. You thought that she would be somewhere else." Pode nodded. "You had information that she might be somewhere else, in fact. So, if I said that you had rung her up at Felcliff and asked her to meet you late that night, I would be mistaken."

"You'd be completely mistaken."

"I see. And you can assure me of that, though you are supposed to have no knowledge of your movements that day. You are also supposed to have suspected nothing about your wife's affair with Wayne till Star and Ruth Wayne told you about it. You say that you still do not really believe it is true. Got a cigarette on you, old man? I don't feel like starting up the pipe again." Pode helped himself to Bill's packet and struck a match.

"Thanks!" He blew a smoke ring across the table and smiled; the slow, lazy smile of a cat who knows that the mouse is almost within its reach.

"Now let's see if there is something that you can remember. Do you know what clothes you were wearing at Sedale?"

"Yes, I think I can remember that." The question seemed quite meaningless and unimportant. "A pair of flannel slacks and an old tweed jacket."

"That's right, old boy. Very good indeed! A tweed jacket with leather patches on the elbows and slightly frayed cuffs. A very old friend, I imagine." Pode got up and took something down from the row of pegs beside the bookcase. "This the one?"

"Yes, yes, that's what I was wearing." The time moved back again to nine thirty of a rainy morning and the room became the interior of the Dormobile. He was sitting at his desk looking out at the desolate moorland outside and he was going to start work. The slightly acid smell of Harris tweed from the jacket was mingling with the smell of damp grass and peat from outside. In a couple of minutes he would begin the last chapter of his book, but before he did so he reached into the inside pocket of the jacket and took something out.

"Yes, that's right, old boy. It's coming back at last, isn't it? You took something out of the inside pocket. Let's see if it's there now."

"No, no, it can't be. I destroyed it. I'm almost sure that I destroyed it." As though somebody had taken hold of his wrist and was forcing it forward, Bill's hand groped in the pocket, feeling a notebook, a pen, a crumpled envelope.

He pulled out the envelope and laid it on the table. The address was typewritten, but somebody had crossed it out and written in ink, "c/o The Post Office, Sedale, Derbyshire."

"Yes, a simple enough mistake." Pode took it from him and pulled out a single sheet of paper. "This was posted to your wife, but Mrs. Carver, an intelligent but badly educated woman, mistook the "Mrs." for "Mr." and sent it on to you. It must have come as quite a shock when you read it. No, old boy, you didn't learn that your wife was Wayne's lover this morning. You knew it on the day she died. Look for yourself, though."

"Yes, yes, I suppose I must have known." Bill stared foolishly at the single line of typing and the scribbled signature below it. "Mary love ... Everything taken care of ... Room 301 ... Royal Hotel ... Bath ... Jumbo." He felt his eyes blur and his head start to sink forward, then Pode's hand was under his chin tilting his face up into the light.

"All right, old boy, let's have it, shall we? Though I'm not paid to investigate your wife's death, I want the truth now." There was a sudden brutality in his voice that Bill had not heard before.

"You read this letter and it told you that Wayne and your wife were lovers and had arranged to spend a night together in Bath. We know that you then sat down and changed the ending of your book from a romantic reconciliation to a very nasty murder. And that's all we do know, because you've lost your memory, haven't you?" Pode stood up and stared down at him. All the flabbiness had left his face and he looked what he really was: a tough, efficient old cop who lived for the job.

"Well, let's see if we can refresh your memory," he said. "Let's see if we can fill in those lost hours for you. You know what I'm implying all right, so try and answer my questions." Once again his hand reached out and tilted Bill's face to the light.

"Now, just try and concentrate. After reading that letter and finishing the new ending of your book, did you telephone your wife and arrange to meet her in Felcliff? Did you confront her with Wayne's letter? No, old boy, look at me and tell me the truth." His fingers tightened as Bill tried to turn away his face. "Did you push her in front of that lorry?"

9

King's Cross station just before the start of the evening rush; the lights already glowing in the dark, echoing hall, a locomotive blowing off steam in one of the arrival bays and thin wisps of fog drifting in to join the smoke, steam and diesel fumes. Though it was quiet enough at the moment, there was a sense of expectancy under the calm. Soon the crowds would come pouring up from the Underground and the final effort of the day begin.

"The four fifty-five from platform three. Thank you." Bill took his ticket and change from the booking clerk and looked up at the clock. There were twenty minutes to kill before the Felcliff train left and he turned into the buffet, buying a cup of coffee and carrying it to a table in the far corner of the room, well away from the other customers. His hand shook as he lifted the cup, and from a fly-blown mirror on the wall his face stared back at him. The features were just the same, he supposed, but nobody could call it a handsome face now. There was a heaviness under the cleft chin, the mouth was slack and flabby and there were dark lines beneath the eyes.

But could he have done it? Was it even remotely possible that he had killed Mary? He asked the mirror, and his own face seemed to nod back at him. It was possible all right. Though memory was still closed to him, he could imagine what might have happened. The insane rage after reading Jumbo's letter which had made him change the end of his book, a phone call to Mary at Felcliff, a meeting just before midnight with the damp winds blowing in from the sea and nobody about in the streets. And then what? Rage again as she admitted everything, the sound of the lorry rumbling towards them, a hand on her shoulder and— He pushed the cup away from him and stared at the table to avoid the sight of his own face.

"No, I'm not saying that you did kill her, old boy." The memory of Pode's voice merged with the rattle of crockery from the counter and the hiss of the locomotive. "All I'm saying is that you may have done so. We know now that you had a motive, the opportunity and nobody, not even yourself, has a clue to your movements that night.

"And if we assume that your wife was murdered, and I'm almost beginning to believe that that must have been the case, who else could have wanted to kill her?" Pode had paused, waiting for his answer which didn't come, and then nodded.

"Oh, there is another suspect all right. Allan Wayne had two possible reasons for wanting her out of the way. In the first place, your Mary might have refused to be cast off so easily and threatened to make a nuisance of herself. Secondly, when she heard that Witzleb's papers were missing, she was bound to have put two and two together and things would have been very awkward for him to say the least.

"Yes, Mr. Wayne had two good motives for getting rid of Mary and it wouldn't be difficult. He would know the schedule of the lorries and it would have been easy for him to persuade Mary to take the midnight train; so that they could travel to London together perhaps. All he would need was the strength for one little push . . . ."

No, Bill didn't see that. He couldn't imagine Jumbo having that sort of strength. He might betray his firm and his family, he might have discarded Mary if Ruth had threatened him, but he couldn't picture him having the guts to kill anybody.

But what was Pode really up to, if it came to that, and who were these mysterious principals he said he was working for? The police rejected the idea of Mary having been murdered, so why did Pode seem so certain about it and, apart from the possible coincidence of Caplin's death, what information had he got to support his theory? Was Pode using him perhaps for some private and possibly sinister purpose? Certainly the man's last statement could imply that.

"There is only one way to prove that you didn't kill your wife, old boy. Find out who did. Go up to Felcliff and see Wayne. Confront him with our suspicions. Make him tell you the whole story about the papers. Even if he isn't a murderer, you've still got a lot of questions to ask him."

And Bill was going to do just that. Pode might be using him for his own ends, but for the time being he was going to trust Pode and do what he said. He had to talk to Jumbo or go mad.

"The train now standing at platform three is the four

fifty-five for Peterborough, Grantham, Bradford, Felcliff-on-Sea..." The voice on the loudspeaker broke wheezily into Bill's thoughts and he put down his unfinished coffee and went out. As the door of the buffet closed behind him, he saw a group of men coming through the main entrance and moved hastily to the bookstall. There would be an acquaintance on the train, it appeared. A porter with a trolley laden with custom-built suitcases came first, a chauffeur bearing a rug next and behind them three men in dark suits. Two of them looked like ordinary business executives, but the man in the centre towered over them and from his expression he might have owned the station. Sir Norman Star on his way to inspect the firm's progress.

Bill had no desire to talk to Star at the moment. A few minutes after Pode had left the flat, the man had rung him up and he could still remember the conversation almost word for word. "I see, Mr. Irwin," Star had said, after he had told him that the papers were not in the flat. "You have searched thoroughly and you didn't find them. Thank you for trying, anyway, and I will just have to look elsewhere." He had paused for a moment, as though the connection had been broken, and when he spoke again his accent had sounded much more foreign.

"Mr. Irwin, I believe you to be a perfectly honest man who is telling me the truth when you say that you have no idea where your wife might have hidden our papers. But if you are not—if you have any idea at all where they could be and for some reason are refusing to tell me, I warn you that you may be running into very great danger indeed.

"Good-bye for the present, Mr. Irwin, and our accounts department will be in touch with you about the compensation for the death of your wife."

They were almost up to him now and behind his back he could hear the porter's trolley squeak for lack of oil. Bill bent over the books on the counter. *The Race to the North. Trains We Have Loved. The Gresley Pacifics.* Bright dust jacket showed gleaming locomotives and tall viaducts and Victorian stations with silk-hatted officials handing ladies in crinolines into carriages, and at the end of the row was a book which he felt he should read. It was a thick pamphlet with the arms of the South Riding County Council stamped on the cardboard cover. *The Felcliff Harbour Scheme—A Drastic Remedy.* He handed half a crown to the assistant and glanced over his shoulder. Star and his minions were far down the platform and almost out of sight now. He pushed the pamphlet into his pocket and crossed to the barrier.

It was a long slow journey, the train using a roundabout route, as the direct London to Felcliff traffic was obviously unimportant now, and they seemed to stand for hours at every station it stopped at. Bill shared a compartment with four gentlemen from Bradford and Ilkley who had been attending a wool merchants' conference. They smoked pipes, were provided with an enormous fund of unprintable stories and, though travelling second class, looked as if they would certainly enter "first" on their expense accounts.

The Felcliff Harbour Scheme—A Drastic Remedy. Bill turned on the light above his head and studied the pamphlet. Drastic was the right word, it seemed. A whole town condemned to death to save an area that was dying. There was a map of the South Riding on the second page, shaded to show the density of population, and a graph illustrated the industrial production. The district had the worst unemployment figures in the British Isles and was being slowly strangled for the lack of a modern port to handle its produce.

Felcliff was to provide the port. He turned another page and began to read the details of the scheme. Mary had told him a good deal about it, of course, but he'd never realized how vast the work really was. A town of fifteen thousand inhabitants to be destroyed; its centre demolished to make room for the new docks, the cliffs scooped away to widen the harbour mouth and a narrow salmon river turned into a canal which could handle barges from the industrial areas thirty miles inland.

"Three spades you say, Mr. Cartwright? Ah'll double you then." His companions had settled down to a rubber of bridge which they played with verve and a great deal of noise; slamming the cards down on the table and arguing loudly at the end of each game. "And redouble, Mr. Jenkins."

Yes, Bill could see that it was quite a contract that Norman Star had landed, though he hadn't got it without a fight. The next chapter was headed "Early Opposition to the Scheme," and there'd been plenty of that apparently. Felcliff had been a popular holiday resort with six hotels, one of the finest beaches on the east coast and an ancient monument: the ruins of an abbey which had been built by Richard II. Three newspapers and a dozen organizations had rallied to the town's defence, but government pressure had finally got its way.

"Christ, Harry, why the hell couldn't you have indicated that you had t'ace of clubs? Ah'd have gone three no trumps, if I'd known." The bridge players argued loudly but without apparent rancour, a southbound train rattled past, Bill glanced at his watch. Seven thirty already and they were getting on; Peterborough and Grantham far behind and the flat East Anglian countryside had broken up into low hills with a glow of blast furnaces on the horizon.

"Difficulties Over the Contract." There had been plenty of those too. The whole purpose of the scheme had been to encourage industry in the area, so why hadn't the contract gone to a local concern? The consulting engineer had stated that he could only seriously consider tenders from firms with "proven experience in such works," and in spite of protests from three Yorkshire companies, the South Riding Development Board had backed him up.

The matter hadn't rested there, however. A newspaper had stated that there appeared to have been something of a gentleman's agreement in the way in which Star Construction finally got the contract. Its editor had lost the libel action that followed, but Bill felt that his charges might easily be true. He could almost picture Norman Star smiling persuasively across a table in some very private room and hear his voice. "So that's that, gentlemen. Our figure for Felcliff is to be twenty-nine million, three hundred thousand and both of yours will be slightly in excess of it. In return, Mr. Lampton, there is no need for you to worry about our competition on the Severn Tunnel, nor you, Lord Garratt, when tenders are invited for the Taunton Reservoir."

"Just a minute, Mr. Cartwright." The card player nearest Bill scowled as his opponent spread his hand on the table. "The rest are yours! Ah'm very, very sorry, but I'm afraid I don't see that at all. Oh yes, your king covers my queen all right, but what about my partner's nine of trumps here. That's bound to take your six and leave the way open for . . ." A full-scale argument seemed to be about to develop this time, but at that same moment the train braked hard, clicked over a line of points and came to rest alongside a dismal platform with a voice announcing, "Bradford—Bradford—this is Bradford," as though it were premier city of the world. His companions gathered up their belongings and climbed out still arguing, doors slammed, a whistle blew and Bill was alone at last.

Beyond Bradford the landscape changed again. The little hills solidified into a vast moorland plateau with not a light on the horizon, though the glow of blast furnaces was still visible to the far south. In the past this stretch of country had been ravaged by Saxon and Viking and Norman and they made him think of plundered villages left burning after a raid. The train had divided now, half for Felcliff and half for points farther north, and the diesel had been replaced by a steam locomotive. He could hear it grunt and cough as it struggled up across the moorland.

"I think I can—I think I can—I think I can . . ." The slow, heavy, out-of-breath voice of the machine seemed to become human as he listened to it: to become Pode's voice repeating the questions. "After finishing the new ending of your book, did you telephone your wife and arrange to meet her at Felcliff? Did you confront her with Wayne's letter? Did you push her in front of that lorry?" Bill leaned far back on the seat and closed his eyes. Behind him the grunting voice turned to a whistle as they ran towards a tunnel and then the whistle grew into a scream. The roar of the train in the tunnel might have been the sound of a heavy lorry and his hand on the arm of the seat might have been resting on a woman's shoulder. He suddenly seemed to see Mary's face staring at him with its mouth open to scream again, and then she was falling away into blackness. He was asleep.

"Felcliff—Felcliff-on-Sea—all change here." Bill opened his eyes, took his case from the rack and climbed out of the compartment. He must have remained asleep for some time since the train had arrived, for the platform was deserted except for a couple of porters unloading mail bags and a ticket collector by the barrier. There was no sign of Star and his companions. Probably they were already being driven off to the bungalow village that the firm had built somewhere out on the moors.

He gave up half of his return ticket and walked out into the booking hall. Felcliff station had been very gay once. There was pink strip lighting along the ceiling, the cigarette and confectionery booths were brightly painted, and the walls were covered by posters advertising its attractions as a resort. Two girls in bathing costumes, with long tanned thighs and breasts that looked as though they had been blown up with a bicycle pump, smiling provocatively from a beach of yellow sand. The pier with fishing boats and excursion steamers tied up alongside it. The Royal Hotel, a huge pile of Victorian Gothic dominating the cliff top. The Golf Course, the Botanical Gardens, the Amusement Park and Fun Fair, the abbey ruins. Very much last year's posters, though. At first glance he could see that they were torn and faded and covered with months of neglected soot and dust.

He turned out into the street, smelling salt and seaweed and another smell that brought back memories of the blitz: rubble. The acid tang of shattered bricks and mortar and years-old dust released from attics and cellars. He tightened his coat and glanced down the street for a taxi. There were none in sight and the street was quite deserted. This part of Felcliff might have been a dead town, left to rot on some burnt-out and forgotten planet.

Only this part, though. Towards the sea front there was work in progress. A crane towered over the harbour bearing the huge sky sign of STAR CONSTRUCTION—UP ON TIME from its mast, and beyond it there was a blaze of floodlights. In the glare he could see a steel ball circle and swing from its chain to crash against the wall of a building. Most of the inhabitants had left Felcliff, and the wreckers were hard at work.

"A taxi, sir?" The ticket collector had obviously finished for the night and was on his way home. He looked at Bill as though he had just been asked for the loan of a hundred pounds. "I'm afraid you won't find many of them about these days. Not at this time of night at any rate. Where are you wanting to get to, sir?"

"I want the . . ." Mary had stayed at the North Cliff Hotel. Somehow Bill hated the thought of going there, but it seemed necessary. He might be able to find a waiter or maid who had talked to her.

"The North Cliff, sir. I'm afraid there's no point in that. It closed down just the other day."

"But I knew somebody who stayed there only three weeks ago."

"That's as may be, sir, but it's shut up now all right. Like most of this town, I'm sorry to say."

"Damnation!" Bill swore under his breath and glanced at the posters in the hall. "What about the Royal then?"

"The Royal, sir!" The man shook his head sadly. "If you asked me a couple of weeks back, I'd have said that you couldn't have picked a better hotel in the whole of the South Riding, but you won't get in there now."

"You mean it's closed too?"

"Closed up as tight as a clam since ten days ago, sir. All that part of the cliff's being cut away to widen the harbour mouth. They're supposed to be pulling down the old Royal tomorrow. Making a sort of public show of it, so I've heard."

"I see. I imagine they'll have quite a job." Bill looked at the line of cliff standing out like a rampart against the sky. "Is there any other place near here that might put me up for the night?"

"Well, I dunno, sir. Not much call for accommodation in Felcliff these days. All the construction people are living out at that new village they've built on the moors near Seatoller. You might try the Castle Hotel, though. I did hear that they were keeping a few rooms open. Yes, I'd go along to the Castle, if I were you. Turn left outside here and keep along Ocean Approach and Grand Parade to North Cliff Road. You can't miss it, sir. Take you about ten minutes or so."

"Thank you very much." It would have to be the Castle then. Bill picked up his case and walked forward. Mist and drizzle were mingling with rubble and sea smells, and from the direction of the searchlights he heard a crash of falling masonry as the demolition teams carried out their work. There was a thick layer of mud on the road; greasy mud with a crunch of grit in it that must have come from the loads of rubble being moved out to the dumping grounds. Most of the street lamps were out, but in the thin moonlight he could make out the names of the little hotels and boardinghouses that lined the pavements.

The Pines—The Florida—The Sea View—The Gables— The Halfway House ... Tart images of childhood crept through his mind. Flags in the wind, moated sand castles and vanilla ice cream melting in the sun. Roundabouts whirring in the far distance and the sound of a band playing in the Botanical Gardens. Grey soft-shelled crabs that had been left by the tide in little hollows of rock and seaweed. Spades and buckets dribbling sand beside potted palms in the hallways of dark lodginghouses.

Station Road—Ocean Approach—The Esplanade. Shops that had once sold rock and candy floss, and souvenirs, and comic postcards of stout ladies in bathing dresses, and coy chambermaids in the bedrooms of lecherous guests, and shy honeymoon couples ... all empty now, with grimy windows and signs reading "Closing Down Sale," "Everything Must Go" drooping on the glass.

Grand Parade. A line of tall lamp standards with a ship and dolphin device and a block of flats that had already been half demolished to show the huge rambling pile of the Royal Hotel on the cliff with a Star Construction sign blazing above it.

North Cliff Road. Bill paused and looked at his watch. Ten o'clock exactly. Mary had died just before midnight and this was the place where it happened. Two roads meeting, the station clock just visible in the far distance, a phone booth at the junction and a café named the Winds of the Sea with its shutters up behind it. This was where she had died and suddenly he was no longer afraid. Sadness was still with him, loneliness and anger, but no fear at all, for as he looked around him, he knew quite clearly that he had never been in this place before. Whatever Pode might think, he couldn't have killed her.

He started to walk forward across the junction and then paused as he heard the noise. The rattle and cough of a heavy vehicle being driven fast, but by some trick of acoustics there was no knowing the direction it was coming from. And then he saw it: a black bulk with two tiny sidelights in front, charging down the hill towards the harbour, swinging round the café and coming straight at him. He jumped for his life, feeling mud and grit spatter over him as the lorry clawed at the bend and roared on with the words "Star Construction" clear in the moonlight.

"You bastard!" He stared after the lorry. It was almost at the bottom of the hill already; a ten-tonner by the look of it, and there must be at least fifteen tons of steel girders slung over the tailboard. Fifteen tons and fifty miles an hour on a greasy road with poor lighting! Caplin had been lying all right when he said that he was only doing twenty-five. Star's drivers were obviously on high piece rates, and with few police about in the almost deserted town they felt they could do as they liked. Probably the lack of headlights was a deliberate move to distract attention from their speed.

Poor Mary. That was how she had died all right. Jumbo Wayne had told her that their affair was over and she had run blindly down the hill in front of a lorry which was travelling too fast to avoid her.

And poor Jumbo too, if it came to that. Jumbo probably thought he was in clover now. Safe and snug in the bosom of his family, with a guarantee of a future from Star's rival if Ruth changed her mind and turned nasty. Jumbo Wayne was as responsible for her death as though he had stuck a knife through her heart. Yes, poor Jumbo. He was going to be in for a very nasty interview in the morning. Bill brushed the mud from his coat and walked on through the gloom.

                                    10

The Castle Hotel didn't look nearly as grand as the Royal, but it was still a pretty imposing pile. There were wrought-iron gates at the entrance between a pair of stone pillars topped by carved lions' heads, a wide cobbled drive curved up to a porch that could have done duty as a small chapel, most of the rooms seemed to have balconies and the A.A. and R.A.C. signs swung from brackets at either side of the porch. There wasn't a light to be seen anywhere along the front.

Bill walked up the short flight of stone steps to the door. The place appeared to be completely deserted and closed up, but the door swung open at his touch. If anything the hall looked even darker than the night outside, with the sofas and armchairs and tables turned into vaguely sinister shapes by the gloom. To his right a staircase wound away into the darkness, and the only light came from a little lamp by the reception desk.

He crossed to the desk. It was just like a thousand others in a thousand similar hotels, except that no porter or receptionist stood behind it; a table piled with directories and account books, a mahogany flap served as a counter, a map of the district on the wall and a row of pigeonholes for guests' letters, all of them empty. He rang the little brass bell on the counter and waited. He waited a long time, hearing a clock ticking busily on the wall beside him and somewhere in the distance the rumble of one of Star's hurrying lorries climbing out of the town. He rang again and at last got an answer. Feet sounded on the stairs and a light came on behind him.

"Good evening." The girl stood at the foot of the stairs smiling at him, and at first she reminded him slightly of Mary. A tall dark girl dressed in slacks and a sweater, with long hair falling down over her shoulders. Then, as she came closer, he saw that the resemblance was purely superficial. Mary had had what could best be described as a poised face, a slightly secret face which never gave her thoughts away and which had always fascinated him. This girl's face was open and guileless; far too open. She couldn't have concealed a thing.

"Good evening," he said. "They told me at the station that I might be able to get a room for the night here. If you are closed of course . . ."

"No, we're not closed, though why not is anybody's guess, judging from the amount of business we're doing these days." She crossed to the desk and opened the reception book. "Apparently the town council decreed that at least one hotel must be kept open and the draw fell on us. As it happens we can offer you any one of a hundred and ten rooms. Thank you, sir." She watched him sign the book and closed it without even glancing at what he had written.

"Would Number 5 be all right? It's on the first floor with a balcony and bathroom and I know that the bed has been aired. I'm afraid I can't offer you any dinner, though. With the exception of the hall porter, who is sleeping off a bad hangover after the British Legion meeting, the staff go home at night now and I'm a sort of skeleton crew. I could make some sandwiches if you like."

"Number 5 would be fine and I would like a couple of sand-wiches if it's not too much trouble." Bill grinned slightly. With her tight sweater and slacks the term skeleton was completely inappropriate.

"You're practically on your own here then. Isn't it a bit lonely for you?"

"Yes, a bit, but I don't let it worry me, and there's plenty to do. I've been receptionist, chambermaid, waitress and general runabout since Star's people moved out a fortnight ago. I hated it at first, but one gets used to everything in time." She took a key from the rack and frowned as she handed it to him. "Have you been in an accident or something?"

"An accident!" Bill followed her stare. His brushing-off operations in the street hadn't been too successful and there was a long smear of brown mud down the left arm of his raincoat.

"No, it wasn't an accident, though it easily could have been. I had to jump out of the way of a lorry loaded with steel girders. It sprayed a good deal of mud over me."

"I see." Her frown deepened. "Those lorries of Star's really are the limit. The drivers are all paid on piecework rates and they go charging about the town as though it belongs to them. I suppose in a way it does now, but why the police let them get away with it beats me. Only a few weeks ago one of them knocked down a woman and killed her."

"Yes, yes, I heard about that." Bill turned away his face, but the girl was too full of her complaints about Star Construction to notice his expression.

"And why the council lets them behave as they do is any-body's guess. There are three good hotels in this town which are not due for demolition and all of them should be doing business. Now, simply because Star decided to build that bungalow village for their employees, we're the only one that's still open. And they say that this harbour scheme is designed to cut down local unemployment!"

"I suppose it will in time." Bill suddenly wanted those sandwiches very badly and he was in no mood for general conversation. "Now, if I may, I'll go up to my room and have a quick wash. No, please don't bother to show me the way. Number 5 on the first floor. I'll find it all right. See you in a few minutes." He took the key from her and turned up the stairs.

Like the town itself, the Castle Hotel seemed to be part of a dead empty world. Doubtless it would come back to life again when the harbour works were finished and trade returned, but for the time being at least, there was something horribly depressing and sterile about it. The thick carpet felt damp and sodden under his feet, and the banisters, which had once been polished like glass, had a thin layer of dust clinging to the rails. At the top of the stairs a brass shell case, which was obviously used as a gong, swung from its tripod, but he was probably the only guest who would hear it and a cobweb hung from the Royal Artillery badge. He stared down the long deserted corridor with its lines of closed doors, and for a moment he had the uncomfortable feeling that if he beat the gong the doors would open and the ghosts of forgotten holiday makers and honeymoon couples and commercial gentlemen would come flocking out.

Number 5. A very nice room indeed, or had been till business fell off and the staff had been cut down. The bed stood on a little raised dais with curtains draped over its head, the furniture was imitation Louis XIV with panels picked out in white and gold, and the bathroom was a shiny cave of black tiles with heavy plated fittings which could have done justice to an operating theatre. Everywhere there was the layer of dust and an atmosphere of neglect.

He washed in lukewarm, peaty water and stepped out on to the balcony. To the west the Yorkshire moors stretched as far as the eye could see in an unbroken line, and below him the town looked as though it had recently been blitzed. Most of the area around the fish quay was already clear of buildings and a great scoop had been taken out of the South Cliff to make way for the concrete docks of the new harbour. Lorries and excavating machines were moving up and down it under the floodlights, and once again he realized the importance of the contract that Norman Star had landed. Out to sea the lights of a steamer rose and dipped on the swell, and from the top of the North Cliff the sky sign still flashed above the huge pile of the Royal. He turned back into the bedroom, closed the French windows behind him and went down to the hall.

"Ah, there you are." The girl was laying a plate of sandwiches on one of the tables. "I hope these will be all right. I'm afraid all we seem to have is cheese and ham. Would you like a drink to go with them? That at least I can manage."

"Cheese and ham will be fine and I would like a whisky and soda, if it's no trouble. Perhaps you would join me." He watched her move away to a door labelled Tudor Lounge and turned to the sandwiches. There had been no buffet or restaurant car on the train and he felt extremely hungry. He had almost finished them when she returned with a tray of drinks.

"Those were wonderful." He smiled up at her. "By the way, my name's Irwin—Bill Irwin." Behind the curtains the windows rattled harshly as another lorry clawed up the hill.

"Yes, I know that. I saw it in the book while you were upstairs. I'm Kay Sommers. Cheers!" She sat down facing him and sipped at her gin and tonic.

"Cheers!" Somehow the name seemed to ring a bell, but he couldn't place it for the moment. "You really must have a tough job, running a show like this with only a drunk porter to help you."

"Yes, pretty tough, but three staff come in during the day, so it's not too bad. Besides, the company is paying me a great deal more than the normal salary and it's a question of beggars not being choosers. I've got two small children to keep."

"I'm sorry. That must make things very difficult. No husband?"

"My husband is dead, but there's no need to say you're sorry about it. We were divorced two years before he died and

I was very much the guilty party. I only got custody of the kids because Paul couldn't have cared less about them."

"I see. I still am sorry, though." As he looked into her very open face he saw that it was trying to hide something. Sadness? No, not that. She was speaking the truth and her expression had nothing to do with her husband. What he saw in her face was a mixture of curiosity, pity and something he couldn't recognize. "Poor Kay," he said. Somehow the name seemed to come quite naturally to him. "You've had quite a rough deal."

"No, not especially and, as I told you, it was my own fault." She lit a cigarette and pulled hard at it as though it helped her to control her face and Bill suddenly recognized the third thing that made up her expression. Invitation! Half-remembered techniques and advice from student days came back to mind. Approaches in dance halls, on sea fronts, a sports car being driven slowly into the country with his arm around a girl's shoulder, a beery masculine voice whispering in his ear above the hum of the saloon bar. "No, not that one, old son. Go for the little blonde on the left. The one who keeps laughing and smiles all the time. You can't miss with her—nobody could miss. A nympho—a pushover, if ever I saw one. Go in and win, boy."

"No," she said. "Not poor Kay—poor Bill. I was so sorry about your wife."

"You know who I am?" He craned forward. Had she seen him before, perhaps? On the night that Mary died? Though he hadn't recognized the junction by the phone booth, was it possible that he'd been in Felcliff that evening?

"Oh yes, I know who you are. I thought I'd seen your face somewhere before when we first met, but I couldn't place it. I must have seen it on a book jacket, I suppose. Then as soon as I read your name in the register the penny dropped.

"I liked your wife very much, Bill. She was a lovely woman."

"You knew her?" Even as he spoke, Bill remembered the transcript of the inquest that Carne had shown him and where he'd heard the name before. Mrs. Kay Sommers, aged twenty-seven, widow stated as follows . . . "Mrs. Irwin left the hotel at about eleven thirty p.m. to go to the station. She was returning to Felcliff on the following day and only had a handbag and a small overnight case with her. I offered to telephone for a taxi, as it was starting to rain slightly, but she said that she preferred to walk."

"You worked at the North Cliff?"

"Yes, of course. I've been the receptionist there for almost two years. The same company owns this place as well, and when the North Cliff closed down a fortnight ago they offered me the job here."

"Kay." As he spoke the clock on the wall started to strike eleven and Bill suddenly had the strange feeling that everybody else in the world had died and he and this girl were the only people left alive. "Please tell me about my wife. You were on duty in the hotel that day. What exactly happened to make her change her mind about taking the earlier train?"

"But there isn't anything to tell really. Only what I said at the inquest." Once again he could see that she was trying to hide her thoughts.

"Your wife had a room at the North Cliff for about two weeks. As you know, she was Mr. Wayne's secretary and he was staying at the Royal which is only a couple of hundred yards from us. A lot of the Star executives lived at the Royal till they finished building that bungalow town and moved out there. Your wife was rather a bird of passage. She'd stay a couple of nights with us and then go off for a night; to London, I think."

"Yes, yes, I know all that, but what about the day she died? Can you remember exactly what she did that day?"

"No, not exactly. Everything seemed perfectly normal. She'd been in London the day before, I think, and got to the hotel about dinnertime. In the morning she went to the site office near the abbey ruins, and then she and Mr. Wayne had lunch together at the hotel."

"Wayne had lunch with her? Kay, was it after lunch that she decided to take the night train instead of the afternoon one?"

"No, I don't think so," She shook her head. "Let me try to remember.

"No, it was later than that. Mr. Wayne left about half past two and she went up and packed her bag. She told the hall porter that she'd booked a taxi to take her to the station in time for the five o'clock train to London and that she'd be in the lounge when it arrived. Yes, I remember seeing her there. She was sitting on one of the sofas, browsing through a magazine. Then, just after four it must have been, there was this phone call for her. I took it."

"You took the call yourself?" Bill's hand clenched around his glass. "Kay—the voice on the phone? Could you recognize it? Could it possibly have been my voice?"

"Your voice! But, Bill, I don't understand. I don't understand at all. How could it have been your voice? I mean, if you had made the call surely you . . ."

"Surely I would remember! No, that's the whole point, you see. I don't remember very much of what happened that day. I had some kind of mental blackout and I can't put things together."

"I see. Poor Bill." She suddenly reached out and her fingers took his as another lorry rattled the windows. The invitation on her face was very clear.

"Yes, but the voice, Kay." There was a sudden comfort in her touch, but he had to find out what she knew. Afterwards, perhaps, but . . . "The voice on the phone? Could it have been my voice?"

"It could have been anybody's voice—anybody's at all." She pulled away her hand and shook her head. "It sounded foreign somehow—American perhaps. It might even have been a woman's voice. I didn't give it a thought at the time, but after she was killed I remember wondering if it was disguised. It sounded almost as though somebody had been speaking through a handkerchief."

"A disguised voice. You're sure about that?" That put him in the clear anyway. If he'd called Mary he wouldn't have disguised his voice, he'd have got through as quickly as he could and raged at her. Jumbo Wayne on the other hand? Yes, he was known at the hotel and might have wanted to conceal his identity. "You're quite sure, Kay?"

"No, of course I'm not sure. As I said, it was only after the accident that I gave it a thought. But you need another drink, my dear. We both do." She smiled at him and refilled the glasses. There was something very private and possessive in her smile.

"But afterwards," he said. "After she'd taken the call, what was she like? Upset? Nervous?"

"Upset? No, not at all. Quite the opposite, in fact. She asked me to cancel the taxi and book her in for dinner, as she would be taking the night train. I supposed she seemed a bit tense, but very excited and happy as well. Rather like somebody who thinks she may have won a fortune on the football pools and is waiting to have the news confirmed."

"Happy and excited." The pieces were different but the puzzle was starting to come together. "And you talked to her just before she left for the station, didn't you?"

"Yes, I told them all that at the inquest. At about ten forty-five I asked her if I should order another taxi, but she said she would rather walk. She said that in her present mood she felt she could walk a hundred miles."

"And there was something else, wasn't there?" Bill's fingers took her hand again and his eyes studied her face. "Apart from the taxi there was something that you didn't mention at the inquest. Come on, Kay, I've got to know what it is."

"It was nothing—nothing important at all." She tried to pull her hand away, but Bill held on to it. "Only that we had a drink together before she left. We drank a toast."

"You drank a toast. What was it, Kay?"

"Nothing important. Just to her future. She said that if things went the right way she could look forward to a brand-new future with not a single worry in it."

"And why didn't you tell the police this?"

"Because—because of you, Bill. I didn't know you then, but it seemed the right thing to do. Your wife was dead. There was no point in—Bill, Bill, you're hurting me."

"No point in what, Kay?" He could feel his fingers gripping her hand and pressing it hard against the table. "What did you think she meant by that toast?"

"I thought—I thought . . ." Her face went slack and there was no more fight in it. "I thought—no, I didn't think, I was quite sure—that your wife was going to meet a lover."

Midnight. Cold damp winds blowing in from the sea and somewhere in the distance a clock striking. Bill stood on the balcony of his room and stared out over the ruins of the town. Out to sea another ship was clawing its way northward across the swell, and from down the hill he could hear the rumble of more lorries on their way to the assembly points.

"You bitch, Mary." He murmured the words aloud against the sigh of the wind. "Oh, my God, you silly, greedy little bitch!"

For that was it all right. Kay Sommers's story had confirmed part of Pode's theory, but there was much more to it than that. Mary and Jumbo Wayne had been in the plot together. She had probably been the originator of it, in fact. Mary had always been overfond of money, and it was she who had seen the importance of Witzleb's discovery and realized what a competitor would pay for it.

Yes, it was simple enough. She had told Jumbo Wayne about the papers and he had contacted the rival firm and agreed on a price which would set them up for life.

Silly Mary! Far away down the slope, Bill could see the road junction where she had died and he felt he knew exactly how it had been. Mary had planned to return to London on the afternoon train, copy Witzleb's papers and deliver the copy to the corrupt competitor. Nobody need have suspected her, for two firms might easily have chanced on the same invention. She must have thought she was very clever, but Jumbo Wayne had

had other ideas. Perhaps he was tired of her, perhaps he was afraid she might talk if they ever fell out, perhaps he merely wanted all the profits for himself.

In any case, he had planned accordingly. He had arranged for Star's rival to steal the papers from the flat and he had telephoned Mary and told her that they would travel together to London on the night train. One little push in front of Caplin's speeding lorry and there would be nothing for him to worry about.

Yes, Allan Wayne was Mary's killer all right, and in the morning Bill intended to beat the truth out of him. Just now he was tired, though, very tired. He lit a final cigarette, watching the glow of light from the harbour and the red sign of Star Construction flashing over the cliff by the Royal. The wind rattled the windows behind him and there was a dull crash of falling masonry from beyond the floodlights. Behind his back a board creaked and he heard the click of a latch.

He turned and walked back into the room. Kay Sommers stood in the doorway and in the gloom she almost looked like Mary again, with her long hair flowing over her shoulders, a pale blue dressing gown and the shy smile of welcome. She wasn't his wife, though. She was just a tart. A hungry little alley cat who had walked into a hundred guests' bedrooms in her time. All the same he didn't want to be alone any more.

"So you did come, my dear," he said. "Just as you promised."

"Yes, just as I promised. But, Bill, Bill darling, please be kind to me." For a moment she frowned at his expression and then moved towards him with the dressing gown falling open. Her body was young and firm but the skin looked mottled; branded. Bill drew the curtain and cut off the harsh red beams of light that were causing the brands and came from the sky sign flashing on and off through the darkness—STAR—STAR—STAR CONSTRUCTION—UP ON TIME—

11

There was something very wrong with Allan Wayne. Bill saw that the moment he stepped into his office. In the few weeks since they had last met he had aged and grown thinner. The usually tight, rather florid face was pale and haggard, and his suit hung around him in wrinkles as though the big body inside it had withered like a pupa dead in its cocoon.

"Bill," he said, pulling himself slowly up from his desk like a very old man. "How nice of you to call in and see me." His handshake had no grip at all; a cold formal touching of skin against skin. "But please excuse these rather Spartan surroundings. A bit different from my London office, I'm afraid." The white face forced itself into a smile.

"Yes, I can see that, Allan." Bill glanced around the little bare room. In London, Jumbo had run to Persian rugs on the floor, two Topolski paintings above the fireplace, a cocktail cabinet built into a Jacobean spinet and a desk that looked like a cinema organ with a row of buttons and switches that might have been the control panel of a moon rocket. Here everything was purely functional. A plain wooden floor supporting a steel filing cabinet, a desk, two bentwood chairs and a table piled with maps and papers; half of one of the prefabricated huts that had been spewed out on the South Cliff to provide the local nerve centre of Star's operations.

"Thank you." Bill sat down in the chair Wayne pulled out for him. This man might have murdered his wife and he intended to get the truth out of him. For the time being, though, he was going to play him very carefully. "As I told the girl in the reception office, I happened to be in the district and thought I'd like to look you up. It's good of you to spare me the time. I imagine you must be pretty busy with all this." Through the window, about a couple of hundred yards away, he could see what was left of the abbey ruins. The bell tower still stood, but cables stretched from it to a bulldozer farther down the slope.

"Yes, I'm busy enough, but I'm still glad to see you, Bill." Wayne paused as the engine of the bulldozer burst into a roar, the cables tightened and the tower began to sway, buckle and finally poured out in a flood of broken stones and mortar, leaving a tall dust cloud drifting away into the sky. Bill remembered the pamphlet he had read on the train. "Partially destroyed by Henry VIII and Cromwell—shelled by a German battle cruiser during the First World War." Now Star Construction had put paid to it. Wayne's voice broke into his thoughts.

"Besides, I wanted to talk to you, Bill. As you know I wrote you a letter, but I'd like to tell you in person how very sorry I was about Mary. She was much more a friend than just a secretary."

"Yes, I know that, Allan." As Bill watched Wayne's face he saw that though Jumbo might have lost weight, he hadn't lost his acting abilities. There really did seem to be great sorrow in his face. Perhaps there was. Perhaps Jumbo really had been fond of her in his way.

"But I'm afraid I haven't just come to pay you a social visit, Allan," he said. "I suppose that the police and probably your father-in-law told you about my being attacked in the flat and having a mental blackout afterwards."

"Yes, I heard about it and I'm very sorry, Bill. Cigarette?" Wayne pushed a box across the desk and reached in his pocket. He didn't bring out a lighter or matches at once, but seemed to be hoping that Bill would do so first. "You must have had a very bad time, I'm afraid. First the burglar and then the news of Mary's death. Enough to unbalance anybody."

"Yes, it was a bad time, but I think I'm through it now." Bill leaned forward as at last Wayne produced a lighter. He then knew why Wayne had hesitated in bringing it out: his hand was trembling and shaking as though he were suffering from some nervous disease.

"I've come to see you, Allan, because I want to know a lot more about Mary's accident. You were up here in Felcliff when it happened, weren't you? Thanks." He took a light from the quivering flame.

"Yes, I was up here, but I can't tell you any more than what came out at the inquest." There was still nothing but sympathy in his face. "As you know, Mary had been in London and I'd asked her to come back here about the revised plans for the demolition program. There's been rather a flap on, as it happens. The American Met. Office has reported the possibility of an early cold spell in December which may bring frost. We have to speed up the whole schedule and finish pouring our first concrete before the end of this month."

"I know about that, Allan. I read your evidence to the coroner. Mary came up here and spent the night at her hotel. In the morning you went through the revised time schedule with her. You lunched together and she was due to return to London with the plans by the afternoon train. That's correct, isn't it?"

"Yes, of course it's correct. I said all that at the inquest." There was more than just sympathy in Wayne's expression now, and a little nervous tic twitched under his mouth. "But why—why are you asking me all this now?"

"Because I want to know the answer, Allan—the real answer." Bill felt his hands clenching together and he fought back the temptation to get up and place them around Jumbo's throat, kneading and twisting the truth out of him. "You had lunch with Mary, leaving her at two thirty, and she was intending to catch the afternoon train to London. Well, why didn't she take it, Allan? Why did you telephone her just after four and tell her to take the night train instead?"

"But I didn't, Bill. I swear that I didn't." Wayne pushed back his chair and stood up. "You think that I phoned Mary at her hotel and told her to get the later train?" A slight strength seemed to have returned to his face.

"Bill, old man, I'm sorry about everything. About Mary,

about the burglar at your flat, but if you think I phoned her that afternoon or had anything to do with her death you must be crazy. I swear—no, I don't have to swear, I can prove it to you." His hand moved towards the switch of the intercom on the desk and then stopped as its bell rang. "Miss Symonds," he said, "I'd like you to come in here for a few minutes, please."

"Yes, of course, sir, but ..." The woman's voice sounded flustered. "The fact is that ..." She broke off and another voice took over; a thick, muddy voice with a rasping whine in it that sounded like rotten canvas being torn apart.

"Wayne? Hans Witzleb here. I want to know why the hell you haven't informed me that all the security precautions have been checked and agreed by the local authorities?"

"I'm sorry. Their okay only reached me a few minutes ago." Wayne almost cringed in front of the machine. He might have married the boss's stepdaughter but at least one member of the firm seemed to treat him with scant respect. "Everything is in order and I have the papers confirming our arrangements as satisfactory here now. I'll have them sent along to you."

"No, no, don't bother. I'll come over and check them myself. *Gott!* Don't you realize that we've got less than fourteen hours to go? Can nobody obey orders in this blasted country? I'll be over right away."

"Yes, yes, of course." Wayne muttered half to himself and half into the intercom. Then he looked up at Bill.

"But what was I saying just now? Yes, that I never phoned Mary that afternoon—that I can prove it. I can, you know, old man, but not just at this moment. Perhaps you could come round to my bungalow at Seatoller this evening. You are staying at Felcliff, I suppose? Good, I'll have a car pick you up at the hotel just after dinner. Eight o'clock all right? See you about half past then." He held out his hand and started to smile. "And Bill, I promise you that I never made that call." In front of him the door burst open and the smile faded.

"So you have a visitor." Hans Witzleb paused in the doorway and stared at them through thick, rimless glasses. He wore leather shorts, a leather jerkin and there was a shooting stick slung over his arm. Bill turned and looked at him with purely professional interest. The man was part of history, though on the surface he looked almost comical. The popular caricature of a Prussian Unteroffizier in mufti, a minor part of the "Captain from Köpenick," a petty government official dressed for a walking holiday in the Black Forest. His short legs were covered with gingery hair and looked as though they had been designed to strut, his chest bulged against the jacket and his bald head was flattened like an egg that had been pinched in at the top.

Yes, on the surface Witzleb appeared almost comical, but his record was impressive all right. Designer of three Bavarian autobahns before he was twenty-five. Government inspector of all German civil engineering works before he was thirty. From 1943-45, chief engineer of Organization K, and answerable only to Albert Speer and Willi Frenzel in person. A frequent visitor to the Berlin bunker till the Red Army cut off the city. One of the last men to have seen Adolf Hitler alive.

"Mr. Irwin is just leaving. See you soon after eight then, Bill." Wayne started to move to the door, but Witzleb raised his arm.

"*Ein* moment, *bitte.* You say Mr. Irwin? Mr. William Irwin?" His glasses swung over Bill and he nodded approvingly as though he had just discovered an interesting and possibly valuable object that he wished to examine.

"Mr. Irwin, I wonder if you would be kind enough to spare me a few minutes after I have finished in here. I think we have one or two things to say to each other and I would appreciate it if you would."

"Yes, if you wish, but I don't see . . ." Bill winced slightly as the German squeezed his hand. How many death warrants had it signed, he wondered? How many lives had that little smiling face nodded into oblivion?

"You will see, Mr. Irwin. Believe me, it is necessary that we talk. Now, if you would excuse me for a couple of minutes, please." He bowed to Bill's nod and marched—that was the only way to describe his strutting walk—to the desk where Wayne was unrolling a map.

"Now, Mr. Wayne, let me have a look at the security arrangements which you have prepared for tonight." The Mr. was obviously an unusual courtesy put in for Bill's benefit. "They had better be very thorough as I think we may expect a large crowd to see the fun.

"No, no, please don't explain them to me." He cut Wayne short as he started to speak. "If I cannot take them in at first glance, those fools of police won't be able to follow them in a hundred years.

"You have a four-foot-high barbed-wire fence stretching from the top of the cliff here—to the main gates here—to the side gate—and right down to the beach on the other side. Good!" He pulled out a pencil and scribbled a line of crosses on the map.

"Yes, on each gate and at the firing position, here—here—and here there will be guards provided by the local police. I presume that all these points will be connected by telephone just in case any fools try to push through the wire to get a better view?"

"Yes, of course. They are also going to patrol this line around here with dogs. The floodlight battery will be over by the main gates and I understand that you are having the hotel lights connected as well. Personally I think that's a needless piece of publicity, but if Sir Norman wants it . . ."

"Do you, Mr. Wayne? Do you really think so?" Witzleb's pencil tapped sharply on the desk. "Perhaps you are right, but we must humour our employer's whim. After all, I am merely the construction engineer who is paid to obey orders and you are . . . ?" He broke off for a moment and stood frowning at Wayne through his glasses. "Ah, of course, the boss's son-in-law. I had forgotten."

"Now, what have we got? A wire fence, guards at the gates and firing point, patrols with dogs and loudspeakers to give warning before we blow her. That should be adequate, I think, but one point worries me slightly. The lower face of the cliff here. You haven't allowed for any patrol round it?"

"No, it didn't seem necessary. I spoke to the chief constable a few minutes ago. He said he couldn't allow us any more men, and if anybody was mad enough to try and climb the cliff face we had his full permission to blow him up; that in fact we'd be ridding the community of a dangerous lunatic."

"What?" The German frowned, and then his face twisted into what might be described as a smile, if you had a lot of imagination. "Ah, a joke, the famous British sense of humour which we foreigners are supposed to be unable to understand.

"Very well, we'll let that go and everything else appears to be in order. Have copies made and send one of them over to my office as soon as you can." As though Wayne had suddenly ceased to exist for him, Witzleb turned away from the desk and nodded to Bill.

"Well, that's that, Mr. Irwin. Now, would you be kind enough to come with me?"

From the window of Witzleb's office, Felcliff was like a toy model of a town that had been strewn out on the floor and discarded by children. Most of the shopping centre was gone now, with here and there the wall of a building standing out like a wartime ruin, and by the fish quay there was nothing except an empty brownish-grey rectangle with an endless procession of machines moving across it. On the breeze there came the rattle of air hammers and the thud of steel balls against masonry. Even as he watched, Bill saw the side of a house collapse and fall forward.

"*Wunderschön!* Beautiful, isn't it, Mr. Irwin? I have always felt that there is something very fine about destruction." Glee twinkled in Witzleb's eyes behind his thick glasses.

"This is nothing, of course—a very little operation. In Berlin at the end of '44 one could drive through nothing but rubble all the way from Tiergarten to the Alexanderplatz.

"But this is different. Here we are destroying so that we can—can construct again." His English was educated and accurate, but here and there he had to struggle for a word. "Here we are tearing down the old and worn out and soon we will lay steel and concrete which will last as long as the Pyramids. Below us, where perhaps twenty fishing boats used to tie up, there will be an oil refinery employing more than ten thousand people. On the north bank, instead of that cliff, there will be docks to take ore carriers of over thirty thousand tons dead weight. Does it not excite you, Mr. Irwin?"

"Yes, I suppose so." Bill studied the man as he talked. He had been with Witzleb for over five minutes now and he had told him nothing of what he wanted to speak to him about. He had taken him to the window and pointed out the work in progress, as though he were a friend or a potential client whom he wanted to impress with the firm's capacity.

"And that comes down tonight?" He stared out across the river. On the top of its cliff, the Royal Hotel looked quite indestructible; a huge Gothic castle with its towers and turrets and buttresses; the last bastion to be holding out against the raiders.

"Yes, all that part of the cliff is to go tonight. It is—how do you say?—an emergency. Normally we would pull the buildings down bit by bit and salvage what we could, but now we have no time. The American Meteorological Office has warned us that a freak cold front may be approaching at the beginning of December, and we have to move fast. As you probably know, cement will not set properly in frost and we must pour our first concrete foundations before the weather breaks. Instead of normal demolition methods, we blow her up." He lifted his shooting stick and pointed at the base of the cliff.

"Just there—under that point of rock that looks rather like a human nose—there are three caves running into the cliff. We have extended them with tunnels, and placed explosive charges in each. At exactly midnight tonight, we press a switch and *pouff!* What is the saying? Yes, 'Down comes baby and cradle and all.' It should be quite a spectacle."

"I'm sure it will be." Farther away down the lower slopes of the cliff Bill could make out the Castle Hotel. It seemed to be very small and unimportant compared to the Royal, but he looked at it with great affection as he remembered Kay Sommers. The scent of her in the darkness, the kindness of her, her hair spread out beside him like black flames on the pillow as the morning light crept across the room. He knew that he'd meant nothing to her except a physical experience and that she'd done the same thing a hundred times before, but she'd given him back a lot of confidence and he would always be grateful to her.

"But won't it be dangerous? Didn't you have a job getting the council's permission to bring it down like that?"

"We had some slight difficulty getting permission, Mr. Irwin, but my employer, Norman Star, is a very persuasive man. There will be no real danger either, providing the crowds who come to watch are kept behind the barriers. I am a German and we plan things accurately. The weight of the charge has been worked out to the last ounce. I presume that you are staying at the Castle as it is the only Felcliff hotel still open. I think I can guarantee that not one of its windowpanes will be broken." The hut shook as a huge red bulldozer climbed up the slope towards what was left of the abbey ruins. Witzleb nodded approvingly.

"Nice, isn't she, Mr. Irwin? Very nice indeed! The latest model from Detroit. Somebody, Clemenceau I think it was, said that America is the only nation that has passed from barbarism to decadence without an intervening period of culture. He may be right, but there is nothing barbaric or decadent about their machinery."

"Herr Witzleb." Bill suddenly realized that the man had been talking generalities to give himself time to study him. "Could we come to the point please? Just what is it you want to say to me?"

"Ah yes, of course. By all means let us get down to business, though I would have thought you could have guessed what I want. The papers that I entrusted to your wife. I gather that you did not find them in your flat?"

"No." Bill shook his head. "But surely Sir Norman told you that. I spoke to him on the telephone yesterday."

"Yes, he told me, Mr. Irwin, but I thought I would like to ask you myself." Witzleb took off his glasses and polished them against the sleeve of his jacket. Without them his face seemed to shrink, as though the thick lenses were part of his personality.

"Very well, I accept your assurance that the papers are no longer in the flat. So where are they? Did your mysterious assailant find them, perhaps? From our information that seems unlikely. Could your wife have placed them elsewhere for safe keeping? In her bank or with a friend maybe?"

"No, I didn't think it was very likely but I checked with the bank. She'd deposited nothing with them. Besides, I thought she'd told you that she'd left them in the flat when Jumbo asked her to come up here?"

"Jumbo? Oh, you mean Mr. Wayne, of course." The spectacles were cleaned to Witzleb's satisfaction now and he replaced them. Once again his face looked strong and rather sinister.

"Yes, she told me that and I'm afraid we must assume that they were in the flat at some time, but have since been removed. Now, may I ask you another question, Mr. Irwin? Just what is your reason for coming up here to Felcliff?"

The reason? To find out how Mary died? To revenge her? To know what really happened? He couldn't even be sure of the answer himself, but it was no business of Witzleb's. Bill almost started to tell him so and then changed his mind. There was no point in making an enemy. "I came here to see Mr. Wayne on a private matter," he said.

"Yes, of course, about your wife. Very understandable and I sympathize with you." Witzleb stared out of the window with the sunlight glinting on his glasses and the leather jerkin and showing up the gingery hairs on his legs.

"There is a strong suspicion that your wife and Wayne were lovers. How natural that you should wish to have it out with him. That is no concern of mine, but there is another possibility why you might have come to see him, I think. Norman Star told you that he thinks Wayne may be connected with the man who broke into your flat. He also told you that Wayne could have contacted one of our rivals who would pay a great deal of money for my invention. We can prove none of this, of course, but the fact remains that the papers are missing. I am wondering if you—if—if . . ." Witzleb suddenly broke off into a whisper and something started to happen to his face. Under his deep tan it took on a slightly greenish tinge, and the lips drew back to show a line of badly stained teeth. "The brutes," he said. "Look at the filthy brutes." For a moment Bill thought he was about to have a stroke.

"Herr Witzleb," he said. "Are you all right?" In spite of the revulsion he felt for the man he took his arm. Under the thick jacket the muscles were tensed as though he were under shock treatment.

"Yes, yes, I'm all right, but look at them. I told the foreman to see poison was put down regularly—that I would not tolerate them on the site—and I couldn't stand them. And now, outside my own office . . ."

"You mean the rats?" Bill followed his stare. Across the tracks that the bulldozer had left a pair of old brown grandfathers from the sewers were cautiously picking their way towards a broken drain. They squeezed slowly into it, two scaly tails twitching at the lip of the pipe for a moment and were gone. Bill remembered what he had seen in Caplin's flat and shared a little of the German's disgust.

"Sorry. I am very, very sorry." Witzleb turned from the window and pulled a bottle out of the drawer of his desk. "It is—how do you say? Yes, a weakness. I have never been able to stand them and once I saw something . . ." He tilted the bottle to his lips and drank deeply. Almost at once his colour started to improve.

"Yes, I apologize, Mr. Irwin. It is a very childish failing of mine. You will forgive me, please."

"Yes, of course, but there is nothing to forgive." Again Bill studied him with professional interest. A dislike of rats is a common human characteristic, but Witzleb's seemed to be near mania. Just what revolting incident in his past could have given him a horror like that?

"But before you saw the rats," he said. "I think you were about to accuse me of something."

"No, not accuse. That is the wrong word. All I want to do is to warn you, Mr. Irwin. But please let me finish." He raised his hand as Bill started to break in. "To the best of our knowledge those papers were in your flat. If you had found them, and I am not suggesting that you did, they would be quite meaningless to you, and you would not know where to dispose of them. Wayne knows who he could sell them to, however, and so I wonder—I wonder if you might have come up here to make a deal with him."

"And I've had just about enough of this." Bill felt anger rising like a pressure gauge as he listened. "My wife was seduced by Allan Wayne. She was killed by one of your lorries and I'm almost beginning to believe that he may have pushed her in front of it. I came up here to find if that is the truth. Just what do you think I am, Herr Witzleb? Do you think I would make a deal with Wayne after what he's done to me? You must be crazy, and I don't give a damn about your blasted papers. Apart from Star telling me that they have to do with the manufacture of cement, I know nothing about them and I couldn't care less whether you find them or not."

"Good! Very good indeed! That sounds like the truth to me." Witzleb turned from the desk and came towards him. His features were set in a smile, but behind the glasses his eyes were completely dead and cold.

"Yes, Mr. Irwin, for the time being at least, I am prepared

to believe that you have not got those papers. But if, at some
future date, you find out where your wife hid them—if you
forget your grudge against Wayne and even consider making
a deal with him—I warn you ..." Though the top of his
head was barely on a level with Bill's eyes, he felt the power
of the man and remembered his record. Witzleb had been
chief assistant to Willi Frenzel, and Frenzel's name had been
feared almost as much as Himmler's. Could that verdict which
acquitted him of everything except technical participation in
Organization K have been correct, he wondered? Was it likely
that Frenzel would have considered anybody who wasn't as
ruthless and fanatical as himself for such a post?

"Yes, I warn you, Mr. Irwin." His hand came up and gripped
Bill's arm. It looked a small pudgy hand, but Bill could feel the
hardness of the muscles through his sleeve. "Most of my life I
have been a violent man and I haven't changed now. I want to
recover those papers and I will go to any lengths to do so."

12

The papers had nothing to do with the manufacture of
cement! Bill relaxed against the back seat of the car which
was taking him to Wayne's bungalow and he was quite certain about that. Star might have said so—Wayne and Mary
might have thought so—but Hans Witzleb knew differently.
As Witzleb had gripped his arm in the office, he had looked
straight through the thick glasses and seen not merely anxiety
for the safety of an invention in his eyes, but fear. Whatever
the papers really contained it was something that Witzleb was
desperate to recover.

Yes, Bill was very interested in those papers now. Witzleb
was frightened because of them, Star wanted them for financial gain and Pode was somehow connected with them, or
rather the people who paid Pode were. Mary had probably
died because of them. He closed his eyes, trying to picture her

face, but nothing came. The only face he could see was the face of Kay Sommers smiling at him across the hotel bedroom.

And Jumbo Wayne had been after the papers too. Jumbo was also terrified of something. No, he wouldn't even think about Jumbo's part in the story for the time being. In a few minutes he hoped to hear it from his lips.

The car had been climbing for more than three miles now. Beyond the driver's stolid back the moorland stretched away to the west, broken by dry-stone walls, jagged outcrops of rock and here and there a line of grouse butts. Though the road was narrow and winding it carried a fair amount of traffic. Since leaving Felcliff they had passed three heavily loaded buses grinding out to the bungalow village that housed Star's workpeople, and now and again cars and motorcycles slid by them in the opposite direction. Through the rear window Bill could see Felcliff in the far distance; a dull glow of light across the moorland with the evening star coming up above the sky sign by the Royal Hotel.

"Not much further to go now, sir." They had reached the crest of the slope at last, and the driver pointed to the village that lay in the dip beyond. It was made up of rows of prefabricated huts stretching out from a central square to form a four-pointed star, and in the dusk it looked like a prison or a concentration camp.

"Yes, quite a place, ain't it sir? The poor bleeders say that they've got everything to keep 'em happy, but I couldn't stick living out here myself. I told the transport manager I'd either stay with my sister in Sheffield or they could keep the job. I've been with the firm more than ten years, of course, so they let me get away with it."

"I don't blame you." As they approached the square Bill could make out three bigger huts which appeared to be used as a cinema, a supermarket and a social club. Norman Star obviously liked to keep his workpeople under his thumb and he wondered how they stood it. Probably high piece rates and local unemployment were the answer.

"Yes, grim, ain't it, sir? This is just where the herd lives, of course. Higher up the toffs have it a bit better!" The man swung the car up another slope and towards another group of buildings. The toffs did seem to have it a bit better, but not much better. Their bungalows were slightly bigger and painted green instead of the drab uniform brown, there were parking spaces between them and the roofs bristled with television masts, but the same drabness hung over everything. Bill imagined that Witzleb had probably designed the place and deliberately aimed at the concentration-camp effect. It was easy to picture barbed-wire fences and watchtowers and a sign reading *"Arbeit Macht Frei"* above a gate.

"And here we are, sir. This is Mr. Wayne's." The driver stopped the car and leaned round to open Bill's door. "He told me not to wait for you as he'd be running you back to the hotel himself."

"I see. Thanks very much for bringing me then. Good night." Bill got out and walked up the short path to the bungalow as the car reversed, turned, and drove off. Down the street in the herd's area, a motorcycle started explosively, and high up in the sky an aeroplane was droning slowly away to the south. He almost wished he was on it.

"Welcome, Bill boy. Welcome to my castle." Before he even pressed the bell the door swung open and Jumbo Wayne leered out at him. He was obviously very drunk indeed.

"Come in, though. Come in and make yourself at home; if that's the right word for this dump." He stood back and waved Bill through into a little hall-cum-sitting room. It was about as homelike as a prison cell, with functional fumed-oak furniture and curtains that probably divided it from a bedroom.

"Good." Wayne slammed the door behind them and lurched to a table. With his dark five o'clock shadow, bloodshot eyes and a gob of yellowish bile hanging from his chin he was a very unpleasant sight.

"Now for my duty as a host, old boy. A drink after your tiring journey." He picked up a glass and started to slop whisky into it. His aim was pretty bad and a lot spilled on to the table.

"No, I don't think I want to drink with you, Allan. Not just for the moment at any rate. In your office you told me that you could prove you didn't make that phone call to Mary. I came here to hear you prove it."

"Yes, yes, I remember." Wayne turned and grinned at him. "I can prove it all right, but I'm telling you nothing unless you drink with me—nothing at all." He stared down at the bottle in his hand. "Come on, old boy. This is good stuff—the best. Listen to what it says on the label. 'By appointment to Queen Elizabeth II.' If it's good enough for her, it should be all right for you. 'Distilled and bottled in Scotland—Gold Medals at Edinburgh, Paris, Antwerp and . . .' No, I can't read the rest of them. All the same, this is all right. Only had three, or was it four this evening, and I feel like a bloody king already."

"No, I still don't want to drink with you, Allan. Not until you've told me about that phone call." Bill moved back as Wayne lurched towards him. His breath smelled horribly sour and there was a metallic tang merged with the reek of whisky.

"Oh, blast the phone call!" Wayne replaced the bottle on the table and grinned foolishly at it. "Very well, I'll tell you. I can prove that I couldn't have made it. I wasn't near a phone at all that afternoon. After leaving the hotel I went straight out on to the site and stayed there till almost seven o'clock. I was going to get my secretary, Mary Irwin, into the office to tell you that . . .

"Oh, sorry, old boy. Not Mary! Mary's dead, isn't she? I mean my new secretary, Betty Symonds. A very pretty girl that, but a *right cow*, as they say in the north." He paused and took a deep pull at his whisky.

"Yes, I have it on excellent authority that Miss Symonds is having an affair with one of our crane drivers. Not only immoral of her but out of her class as well. A very bad example indeed! Have to speak to her about it, Bill. I never could stand immorality."

"And this Miss Symonds can prove that you couldn't have telephoned Mary that afternoon?" Bill frowned. There was something wrong. Jumbo had a very strong head for alcohol and the bottle on the table was barely a quarter empty. It would have taken far more whisky than that to put him in the state he was.

"Of course she can prove it. That's what I keep on telling you." Wayne took a step back against the table, knocking over an ash tray as he did so. Behind him the curtains swayed slightly as though a window was open in the adjoining room.

"I was going to ask Betty to come into the office and tell you herself, but that bastard came barging in as usual."

"Witzleb?"

"Yes, Hans Bloody Witzleb, may hell be hot for him. Herr Baldur the Beautiful, Buchenwald, Bergen-Belsen; what's in a blasted name? I nearly walked out of the firm when the old man took him on."

"I'm sure you did, Allan. Just as you almost walked out when your wife told you to get rid of Mary."

"What's that?" Wayne steadied himself against the table and took another swig of whisky. "I don't know who told you about that, Bill, but I'll tell you something right now. Either you drink with me, or you can get the hell out of here."

"Very well, I'll have one drink with you, if that's what you really want." Bill took the glass from him. Wayne was too far gone to care about threats, but the hint of good fellowship might persuade him to talk.

"Ah, that's better—much better. Cheers! All good pals again, eh, Bill?" He lifted his glass without noticing that Bill didn't drink. "Now, let's talk, shall we? You say that Mary got a phone call on the day she died which persuaded her to take the midnight train to London. You seem to think that I made it? Why should I do that?"

"I think you had a reason, Allan. Two reasons in fact." Bill started to sip at his drink and then paused, for there was something wrong with it. Something very wrong with it. He could make out a faint, metallic odour mingling with the smell of peat and malt.

"Two reasons? More riddles? Come off it, old man." Wayne fumbled for a cigarette. He seemed to have great difficulty in lighting it, the flame flickering backwards and forwards across his face before he finally managed.

"You're implying that I persuaded Mary to take the later train and then followed her to the station. I think that you'll next be saying that I pushed her in front of that lorry. You're wrong, Bill. God, you're so very wrong! Poor Mary—poor little Mary. I wouldn't have hurt a hair of her head." A single drunken tear ran down his cheek. "But why, Bill? Just why do you think I should do that? What possible motive could I have had?"

"You'd got two reasons, as I said, Allan. In the first place Mary was your mistress. She had been for years. It was probably an arrangement that suited you very well. Then your wife found out about it and told you to get rid of her. If you didn't, you'd have lost your job at a moment's notice."

"So Ruth told you that? The bitch told you that?" The room was lit by a single standard lamp. Wayne lurched towards it, shaking his head, with the light shining on his face—mottling it, just as the sky sign had mottled Kay's body in the hotel bedroom.

"But you don't know what she's been like, Bill, since that damned horse went and fell on top of her. Ruth's sick, you know. Not just in her body, but her mind as well. She's crazy, Bill, quite crazy. Just as old Star is crazy, though nobody seems to realize it." He pulled hard at the cigarette and another tear dribbled down his face.

"No, old man. Mary and I weren't lovers, though it wasn't for a lack of trying on my part. Ruth imagined it all and she put a private detective on to us. The bastard couldn't find out anything, of course, but Ruth didn't believe him. Her crazy mind started to invent the sordid details by itself. And you believed her, Bill. I always thought we were pals, but you went and took

Ruth's word for it, without even having the decency to come and ask me."

"I didn't take Ruth's word for it, Allan. I didn't have to." Bill felt slightly sick at the maudlin use of the words "pals" and "decency." "I knew that Mary was your mistress before I even talked to Ruth. You wrote her a letter, but it was forwarded to me by mistake. Remember what you said, Allan? 'Mary love . . . Everything taken care of . . . Room 301 . . . Royal Hotel . . . Bath.' "

"What! You mean that you had that letter?" Wayne stepped back as though Bill was about to hit him. "It was forwarded to you and you thought it merely confirmed a dirty weekend in Bath. You fool, Bill, God, you bloody fool!" He suddenly looked much more sober and some of the original bounce had come back to his voice.

"No, the letter was about the papers—Witzleb's notes. She gave them to me to hide till she had spoken to Star. We thought we'd got everything taped, you see, and I never imagined they would kill her. Honestly, Bill, I never thought that. You believe me, don't you?"

"I don't know what I believe, Allan, but I think you'd better me everything."

"Yes, yes, of course. I want to do that." Wayne nodded. His back was almost touching the curtain now. "I've wanted to talk to somebody about it for a long time, but I was frightened. I should have gone to the police when she died, but I just hadn't the guts. It was like this, you see. When Mary realized what the papers really meant, we thought we could make money out of them; such a lot of money. She told me to hide them just in case anything went wrong. That was what my letter really meant; that I'd put them in that bathroom at the Royal here. Don't blame me, Bill. We thought we could make such a lot of money." Quite suddenly and without any warning he broke off and his face went completely blank. The glass dropped out of his hand, shattering on the floor, a thin bubbling sound came from his mouth and he swayed back against the curtains. For perhaps five seconds he stood like that with his body bent out as though on an instrument of torture and then he fell forward towards the lamp. As its light went out, Bill hurled himself at the curtains, but he was too late. There was a gap in them now and through it something heavy swung up and beat him down.

13

Very slowly and cautiously Bill opened his eyes. There was a throbbing, but not unpleasant sensation in his head, and he was half-sitting, half-lying on one of the chairs. The standard lamp still lay on the floor with its shade shattered, but somebody had turned on a light by the door.

In front of him Jumbo Wayne knelt at the side of the table with his head sunk against the carpet. He looked even heavier in death; a statue carved out of stone which was waiting to be swung up on to its pedestal and there was no doubt as to what had killed him. The handle of the knife between his shoulders could have been an attachment for the crane that would lift the statue into position.

And beside Jumbo, almost touching his left arm, was a pair of boots. Thick, black, well-polished boots with broadcloth trousers above them that ran up into a sagging belly draped by a watch chain, heavy sloping shoulders and a great grey face which was staring down at him.

"Well, well! In for the kill again, eh, Bill? Getting to be quite a hobby of yours, it seems." Pode shook his head in ponderous disapproval. "Taken another bat on the head as well. Not a bad one, I'm glad to say, and I've patched it up for you."

"You! It was you all the time." Bill raised his hand, feeling a strip of sticking plaster across his forehead. "You killed him?"

"I did what?" Pode snorted in disgust. "Don't be a bloody fool, old boy. I didn't kill your pal here, but I think you may have a devil of a job persuading the local constabulary that you didn't."

"No, no." Like a stage backcloth suddenly parting, Bill's head cleared and he remembered everything. All that there was to remember—right back to the beginning. How he had read Jumbo's letter at Sedale, and how he had driven back to London drinking heavily on the way to try and drown the anger and misery he felt. He even knew why the journey had taken him so long now. That place with the advertisements on the bar counter! Its name was The Creaking Highwayman, and it wasn't a pub at all but a roadhouse with a dinner-dance in progress. He'd hated the thought of going back to the flat, and after giving a substantial tip to the waiter he'd managed to stay on there till after one in the morning. The waiter would be bound to remember him.

"No, Superintendent," he said, "I didn't kill anybody. There was someone hiding in the bedroom while I was talking to Wayne. He stabbed him through the curtains and then laid me out when I went after him."

"I see. That's your version, is it? Not the most original story, but I suppose it's feasible enough." Pode picked up the whisky bottle from the table and sniffed at it.

"Yes, somebody wants to hear what you and Wayne have to say to each other. He gets in here before Wayne returns from Felcliff—probably all these bungalows have standard keys—and dopes Wayne's whisky to put him in the right frame of mind for conversation. Yes, amytal of some form, I should say." He gave another sniff at the bottle and put it down.

"Then, for some reason which we are going to discover, he kills Wayne and taps you on the head. Feasible, as I said, but it'll take some proving." Pode glanced at his watch. "Have you any idea what time it happened?

"Umuhm, about nine, eh, and it's five to ten now. You've been out cold for forty minutes and our mysterious friend behind the curtain will be well on his way."

"Yes, but you, Mr. Pode—" Bill dragged himself to his feet. "Why are you here? Why haven't you rung the police?"

"Quite simple, old boy. I felt it was time I talked to Wayne in connection with my inquiries. I rather hoped you'd have softened him up for me, but I didn't expect to find him dead. The door was unlocked so I walked in. Got the shock of my life when I found you both lying here.

"As to why I haven't rung the police, that's simple enough too. Till we know a lot more it would be most undesirable for both of us. My principals pay me well and I don't want any of my late colleagues in blue stepping in and taking the credit. As far as you are concerned, it would be madness. You've been very neatly framed indeed. Jumbo Wayne, as you call him, was said to be your wife's lover and that gave you a perfectly good motive for killing him. I'd bet my last dollar that that knife belonged to him as well. In fact, you had a motive, a weapon to hand and the opportunity. For the time being at least I think you'd better keep well clear of the police."

"No, she wasn't his mistress." Mary and Jumbo were both dead, but it made him feel much better to be able to say that. "The letter about the hotel room didn't mean what we thought, but was about something quite different. Wayne told me about it before he died.

"But before I tell you, Superintendent, I want to know exactly what your interest is and who you are working for."

"Very well, old boy. 'Needs must when the Devil drives', eh?" Pode shrugged his shoulders and sat down. "I suppose you could say that I am working for the mysterious rivals that Norman Star mentioned. The people who are interested in getting hold of the papers Witzleb is supposed to have entrusted to your wife. Their name is Hamble and Smith of York. A most respectable firm of civil engineering contractors who feel aggrieved that they didn't get the Felcliff contract. They suspected that there had been some rather sinister understanding between Star Construction and certain members of the South Riding County Council and employed me to try and find out what it was. I've almost done so and it is a very nasty bit of bribery and corruption indeed. The trouble is that I needed Wayne's help to prove it. That's why I've been taking an interest in you, old boy. I thought that if you could be persuaded to accuse Wayne of killing your wife he might break down and tell you what really happened. From what you said just now I gather that he did so." He leaned comfortably back in the chair and pulled out his pipe.

"Now, just sit down, Bill, light up a cigarette and tell me exactly what Wayne said to you."

"I see. Yes, I really do see at last." Pode had finished his pipe while Bill was talking and he knocked it out. "So that's how it was, eh? Though your wife was a pretty delinquent girl, I take my hat off to her. She had courage, lots of courage, which is more than can be said for her collaborator." He scowled down at Wayne's hunched body.

"Still, *de mortuis nil nisi bonum*. The fellow has paid for his folly and we can fit most of the story together now. We'll probably never know how your Mary got hold of Witzleb's notes, but I imagine it was by accident as they would never have entrusted them to anybody to type. At any rate, those notes gave the details of Star's dealings with the County Council, but instead of going to the police like a good citizen she told Wayne about it and they decided to make a bit of money. She was pretty fond of money, wasn't she?"

"She was too fond of it." Bill frowned, for that was an understatement if ever there was one. Mary had been far too fond of money. She had loved it, almost worshipped it, dreaded the thought of poverty like a cancer. He could quite understand how she would have acted if fate had thrown the chance of making some easy money in her way.

"Poor little devil! And that piece of carrion was too scared to go to the cops after they killed her." Once again Pode scowled down at Wayne's body. "In case anything went wrong Mary gave him the papers to hide. He did so and told her where he'd put them in the letter which Mrs. Carver forwarded to you by mistake. They thought they'd taken care of everything, but they didn't realize the kind of people they were up against.

"Oh yes, she was killed because of blackmail all right. As I see it, she must have told Star that she had enough evidence to send him up on a bribery charge and demanded a lot of cash to keep quiet. Star stalled her and told Witzleb to take care of things. At this stage he had no idea that Wayne was involved and probably thought that the papers were bound to be in your flat.

"The rest is simple enough. To a man like Witzleb her death would have seemed the obvious solution. He telephoned her and asked her to travel with him to London on the night train so that they could discuss terms."

"And then he pushed her under that lorry?" Bill felt his hands tightening against the arm of his chair.

"That's right. Witzleb pushed her in front of Caplin's lorry and Caplin had been well bribed to be slow on his brakes. Probably the swine didn't even know who paid him. My guess is that he would have received an anonymous letter containing a bundle of notes and a promise that a lot more would be forthcoming if he did what he was asked. All the same, our friends are careful people and they didn't take any chances that Caplin might talk at some future date. Killed by a gang of lorry thieves indeed! So much for that little fool Angus Macbeth. It's high time he was back pounding a beat, and if I have any influence that's just what he will be doing in the near future.

"But what a fool I've been if it comes to that. Like you, I thought that Wayne's letter was confirming an assignation at Bath, when all the time, right under our noses, it told us where he had hidden the papers." As though to drive home the point he blew his own nose loudly and violently.

"What fools we've both been!" Bill stared at him through the smoke of his cigarette, still not entirely believing the story. Norman Star appeared to be a sane man. It seemed incredible that he and Witzleb should have left those vital documents lying about. It was also incredible that he should have risked three murders merely to conceal evidence of bribery.

"But we'd better be getting on our way, old boy." Pode consulted his watch and stood up. "The sooner the evidence is in our hands the better. Room 301 at the Royal Hotel at Felcliff, eh? Hidden somewhere in the bathroom. Let's hope that we can find them."

"But just a minute!" Bill started as he remembered what he had heard that morning. "You mean you don't know—you haven't heard what they intend doing? That at exactly midnight they're going to bring down the Royal with high explosive?"

"They are going to do what?" A dark flush crept across Pode's face as Bill told him.

"I see. No, I hadn't heard that, so we'd better hurry, hadn't we? We've got rather less than an hour and a half to find those papers." He tightened his coat and moved across to the door.

"Come on, Bill, let's go. If we don't get there in time, we'll have no evidence at all, and we'll both be in trouble—real trouble. My reputation will go for a Burton and you—you, my friend . . ." He pulled open the door and leered at Bill. "Yes, even with our present absurd laws regarding capital punishment, I wouldn't be at all surprised if you hanged."

Like its owner, Pode's car was very large, very old and extremely cantankerous. It had probably once been described by its makers as a limousine, but had been turned into a monstrosity. The front bumper hung loose, the inside wing was cut and crumpled to show it had once met an object as solid as itself, and all along the body scars of battle showed on the unpolished paintwork. It could have been an exhibit in a war museum. "Military vehicle found on the Normandy beachhead, demonstrating the effects of machine-gun fire."

It was easy to see how it had got into that condition, for Pode drove with a complete lack of consideration. Mercifully the bungalow town seemed deserted; probably its inhabitants had gone to witness the demolition of the Royal, but he shot round the square as though on a race track, missing a lamp standard by inches and over-revving the engine as he charged up the slope. The old car lurched and swayed and screamed on the uneven road surface which had already been chewed up by its unaccustomed flow of traffic, but Bill hardly noticed it. He sat hunched in his seat, staring blankly at the facia board as Pode filled in the rest of the story.

Somehow, by chance or accident, Mary had got hold of Witzleb's notes; those very private papers which had nothing to do with any new form of cement, but proved that Star and Witzleb had got the Felcliff contract by bribery. £15,000 for the Consulting Engineer to the South Riding Development Board and £10,000 each for three of the more vocal County Councillors were the figures Pode considered likely. Probably the notes were in some form of code, but Mary had realized what they meant and her pathological fear of poverty had told her what she should do with them. She had taken Jumbo Wayne into her confidence, asked him to hide the papers, but she hadn't realized that Jumbo was a man of straw who would back her up if things went well, but would be too terrified to do anything if they didn't.

And then she had set out to blackmail Star and Witzleb, forgetting that Witzleb was a very hard citizen who probably had many deaths to his credit already.

No, one more murder wouldn't have worried Hans Witzleb and the means were simple. An arrangement with a corrupt lorry driver whose route and time schedule he knew. A phone call to Mary at the hotel, telling her to meet him outside the station so that they could travel together on the night train and discuss her demands. One little push and he would be free to go on to London and search her flat for the papers.

"Ah, here we go! Now we'll see what this old girl will really do." They had topped the slope now and Pode changed into fourth gear, glancing at the dashboard clock as he did so.

"Yes, an hour and twenty minutes to zero. I suppose they will have all the ground around the hotel pretty well cordoned off." He frowned as Bill told him what he had heard.

"Yes, I imagined the arrangements would be something

like that. Guards on the gates and barbed-wire right round to the face of the cliff. We've two alternatives then: to try to get through that wire, or spill the beans to the local cops. Don't like that, but if their cordon is as tight as you say, it may be our only way. Anyway, let's take the fences as we come to them." His foot came hard down on the accelerator and the old car breasted the hill and roared forward. Its worn engine bearings rattled in protest, the rusty springs bucked and heaved on the tarmac, but the power was there and there was a lot of gravity to help it now. The moorland and rocks flew past them through the windscreen and the speedometer needle jerked up into the fifties, the sixties, the high seventies, hit eighty and held it.

Yes, Hans Witzleb had killed Mary all right, and with Caplin well bribed it would have been easy. Bill struggled to concentrate against the lurching of the car. Just one push as the lorry rounded the bend and a short walk to the station and the midnight train which would get him to London by three fifteen. Then a taxi to Richmond—say thirty minutes, with the streets deserted at that time of night. Just enough time to have searched the flat before he came home and surprised him.

"Take it easy!" He looked up with a jerk as the car quite literally took a bend on two wheels, scattering gravel like spreadshot behind it.

"What's that? Getting nervous, old boy?" Pode cackled with near-senile glee. "No need for you to be. In the old days I was considered to be one of the top Flying Squad drivers. Besides, we're in a hurry." He hunched forward over the steering wheel as another bend loomed up in front of them, swinging the car at it in an expert racing glide with the rear mudguard narrowly missing a jagged outcrop of rock as he did so.

"If those barriers round the cliff are as efficient as you say, it's going to take us a bit of time to get through them." The road straightened, he accelerated again and they roared on down the hill.

"Yes, I suppose you're right, but all the same—" Bill broke

off, staring openmouthed down the beam of the headlights. "Look out—for God's sake, look out! Can't you see them?"

"See what? Damnation!" The grin left Pode's face and his foot came down on the brake. In the distance, two hundred yards away but closing rapidly, a party of sheep were blocking their way. Two, three, four solid mountain sheep moving slowly across the road as though it belonged to them and quite unaware of the death that was hurtling towards them at seventy miles an hour.

"Get the hell out of it." Pode slid the car into third gear, but it still shot down the slope like a toboggan on the Cresta Run.

"Stupid, boneheaded bastards!" His curses mingled with the scream of tortured rubber as the wheels tore at the verge. Almost miraculously the sheep flashed past them unscathed, the road widened into a lay-by and he smiled again. Only for a moment though. The road curved, and they both saw that their escape had been merely temporary for the lay-by was occupied. Right in front of them was a shape. A huge black shape with the glint of polished brass shining in the moonlight and something that looked like a battering ram in front of it. There was no chance of avoiding an accident this time. Bill braced himself against the seat and stared at the speedometer. Forty-five—forty—thirty-five—the car lurched over a boulder, a tire burst, but they still shot forward. Thirty, twenty-seven, twenty-five—-the seat reared up, throwing him against the facia, there was a noise of tearing, twisting metal that seemed to go on for hours, they spun round and the car came to rest, broken and lifeless, under one of the County Council's road rollers which had been parked in the lay-by for the night.

"You all right, old boy?" Pode was staring down at him and at first glance he appeared to be covered in confetti. Then as Bill's eyes grew accustomed to the darkness, he saw that it was fragments of safety glass from the shattered windscreen that had showered on to him.

"I think so." Apart from a bruise on his shoulder where he had been thrown against the door pillar and a long tear in the sleeve of his jacket, Bill seemed to be in working order. "Yes, I'm all right," he said. "What about you?"

"Umhm, I'm not sure yet." The driver's door had burst open and Pode climbed stiffly out. "No, there don't seem to be any bones broken." He brushed the glass from his clothes and scowled at the roller.

"Bloody fool place to leave it! Somebody will get it in the neck for this."

"Will they?" Bill resisted the temptation to tell him that the lay-by seemed a perfectly reasonable place to park. There was no time for squabbling. "And just what do we do now?"

"I don't know—I just don't know." Pode turned sadly to the ruin of his car. Apart from the shattered windscreen and damage to the bodywork, the front wheels were stuck out like the hands of a watch at ten to two. "This old girl's had it and it must be a good four miles to Felcliff. I can't remember seeing a house or a telephone booth on the way up either. I suppose we'll just have to hope that somebody comes along and gives us a lift."

"Pretty unlikely, I should say." Bill stared across the moor. Except for the glow of Felcliff to the east, there wasn't a light to be seen on any horizon.

"Yes, I agree with you; most unlikely." Pode lifted his wrist and frowned. "And to make matters worse, I've smashed my watch. You got the time on you, old boy?"

"Yes, it's almost ten-fifty." Bill looked towards the glow in the distance. One hour and ten minutes to go and the Royal Hotel and all it contained would be blasted into a heap of rubble. Could he make it on foot, he wondered? Four miles? Say thirty-five minutes in his present condition and how long to persuade the authorities to believe his story?

"No, you'd never do it." Pode shook his head, as though he had read Bill's thoughts, then he turned to the roller again and his face brightened. Slung above its drawbar was a rusty bicycle.

"Yes, yes, we still have a chance, I think. A very slim one, but still a chance. The front tire's flat, but you'll have it downhill almost all the way. Blast them though!" He glowered at the lock and chain that held the bicycle in position.

"Still, we'll make short work of that." With surprising agility for his age and bulk, he crossed to the car and heaved open the bonnet. The exhaust manifold hissed pleasantly like a boiling kettle as a stream of water dripped on to it from the cracked cylinder head.

"Yes, this is the boy I want." His hand pulled a pair of wire cutters out of the tool chest and a moment later the bicycle was free. He lifted it down from the tow bar and handed it to Bill.

"Right, son. I'm too old for this and it'll have to be up to you now." He reached in his pocket and produced a flask. "Take a pull at that and then get the hell out of here. Find the senior police officer at the hotel gate and tell him that you're working with me. Say that he must hold back the demolition at all costs and send a car out here for me double quick."

"I'll do that." Bill took a deep swig of brandy and handed the flask back to him, flinging his leg over the bicycle as he did so. "Wish me luck," he started to say, but Pode's hand came down on his shoulder and urged him forward.

The bicycle had no light, no brakes and the steering was almost rusted solid. The flat tire lurched and slurred across the rough road surface, but somehow he managed to keep on. After five minutes the chain broke, making further pedalling impossible, but the slope carried him forward fast. At every second the lights of Felcliff crept nearer. He bent low over the handlebars and prayed that he might get to them in time. He made a slightly comical figure with his oil-smeared face, his torn jacket and the raincoat flapping behind him like a scarecrow in the wind.

14

Though the demolished centre of Felcliff was deserted and most of the street lamps were out, the North Cliff was lit up as though for a carnival. The red Star Construction sign still flashed on and off above the Royal, but it appeared dull and unimportant now, dwarfed by the lights of the hotel below it. Hans Witzleb had carried out his employer's instructions to the letter and every window of the Royal was lit up. Norman Star wanted to make the occasion a propaganda stunt for his firm and he was certainly getting his money's worth.

Bill left his now useless bicycle where the slope down from the moors ended and ran up the hill towards the cliff. There were cars parked against the curb here and there, but no people in sight, though in the distance he could hear the sound of community singing. More cars were parked in the drive of Kay Sommers's hotel and there appeared to be a party in progress. Through the hall windows he could see two men in dinner jackets raising their glasses to a blonde girl with a paper cap on her head.

"Oh, my darling—Oh, my darling—Oh, my darling, Clementine—" At each step the singing grew louder, and as the road finally turned on to the top of the cliff he saw the crowd. There were hundreds of people, thousands probably, black under the floodlights and held away from the wire fence by flags and ropes like spectators at an agricultural show. Behind them rows of vans were selling hot dogs and ice cream and there was a lorry with a television camera mounted on it.

"Thou art lost and gone for ever—dreadful sorry, Clementine." The song died and a brisk, confident voice took over on the loudspeakers.

"Now, ladies and gentlemen, I would just like to repeat what

I said a few minutes ago for the benefit of any new arrivals. There is no possible danger, as long as everybody co-operates and keeps well back behind the markers. Please see that you do not crowd forward, and that all children are kept with you. I repeat, there is no danger at all as long as you stay back behind the markers . . ."

Bill elbowed his way slowly through the tightly packed crowd. On the whole its members seemed happy and excited, eager for the promised spectacle, but here and there he heard a note of sadness. "Bloody shame to see the old Royal coming down. Just about the finest hotel the South Riding ever had. Remember the dinner-dances they used to hold? Footmen in livery and a band playing out on the terrace. Why, only last May at the firm's convention I remember . . . Bloody shame . . ."

It seemed to take him hours to make his way to the barrier and all the time the voice on the speakers urged him on. "Just over forty-two minutes to go now, and Sir Norman Star has personally promised me that we shall see quite a spectacle. The caves under the cliff face have been enlarged and charges placed in them; thirty hundredweight of Madelite, I understand . . ." The voice was cut off by the rattle of a helicopter with the words "Courant Newspaper Group" glowing from its fuselage. It hung over the crowd for a moment and then turned out to sea.

"Yes, just exactly forty-one minutes to midnight and then one of Star Construction's engineers will throw a switch and all that part of the cliff from the Royal Hotel to the golf club building will go down into the sea. I won't bore you with the technical details, but as you know it is being removed to make way for the new dock area. Normally the demolition would be carried out by more orthodox methods than this, of course, but the threat of bad weather has made that impossible . . ."

But he was through the crowd at last, squeezing under the rope, with somebody shouting at him. He ran towards the wire fence where a group of men were standing round a steel tripod.

"'Ere, you, sir! Just what do you think you're up to?" A uniformed constable grabbed him by the arm. "Are you deaf or something? Didn't you hear the warnings on the speaker? Nobody's allowed past that rope."

"I know that, Constable, but I must speak to the officer in charge. It's vitally important."

"Well, I dunno about that, sir. Mr. Fenwick is very busy at the moment. Now, just you go back behind the rope like a good chap and I'll tell him you want to speak to him. Here . . ."

He had released his grip slightly and Bill tore his arm free and ran forward towards the tripod. A very tall man in a super-intendent's uniform was talking to one of the Star executives he had seen at King's Cross.

"Yes, of course I've got all that, Mr. Denton. At five to twelve the hotel lights are disconnected. Then, at exactly mid-night, you switch on the searchlights and blow her three min-utes later." The policeman's voice was full of exasperation. "A damn piece of nonsense, if you ask me. Extremely dangerous as well with this crowd tensed up the way they are. Why the County Council or the chief constable gave you permission beats me. I suppose it's this chap Witzleb's idea. Typical piece of German vulgarity.

"Now, just what the hell?" He swung round as Bill touched his shoulder, showing a fierce weatherbeaten face and a little military moustache. "Just who are you? Have you got a pass to come through here?

"What's that you say? Got to stop them blasting? Friend of Superintendent George Pode?" His frown deepened as Bill stammered out his story.

"Well, that's a likely tale, Mr.—Mr. Irwin. Papers hidden in one of the hotel bathrooms! Chap murdered this evening! Car accident out on the moors! Just a minute though . . . !" He leaned forward and sniffed Bill's breath.

"Why, you've been drinking—that's what's the matter with you. You're drunk! Now, just you get back into the crowd and behave yourself, if you don't want to get locked up for the night." He turned to the constable who was standing at Bill's elbow. "Jackson, take this man through the barrier and see he stays there. If he gives you any further trouble, take him in custody."

"But—but, Superintendent—you must listen to me . . ." Bill tried to resist, but the man had already turned his back and the constable's hand was tight on his shoulder. He walked dumbly back towards the rope, seeing grinning faces and hearing tolerant greetings. "Feller's had a skinful . . ." "Tired of life, eh . . ." "Want to get yourself a harp, chum?"

No, there was going to be no help from officialdom. For a moment he thought of appealing to the crowd, but one glance at those grinning faces showed him that that would be just as useless. He pushed through them and looked at his watch. Thirty-eight minutes to go and he was completely on his own. The helicopter rattled in from the sea again and on the television lorry three young men in duffel coats were adjusting their camera.

But there was still a chance. A tiny one, but he had to take it. There were no guards at the bottom of the cliff face. Witzleb had queried that, but the chief constable had said that anybody who was mad enough to try and scale the cliff deserved to be blown up.

Well, he was mad enough to try. Without those papers he could do nothing to revenge his wife and Pode's warning was very clear in his head. "I wouldn't be at all surprised if you hanged."

Thirty-seven minutes! There was no time to think about it any more. He turned and ran down the slope towards the beach. A path led down to it through what had once been a landscape garden with rhododendron bushes and rock plants, and a little stream poured over waterfalls and decorative fish ponds.

And here was the wire. A four-foot coil blocking the path with warning notices strung along it. He looked round for something to press it down and pulled out a rotten wooden post that had once supported a sapling. There was nobody in sight. Everybody, guards and spectators, was up on the top of the hill and the singing had started again. Under the rattle of the helicopter he could hear a hoarse rendering of "Abide with Me."

He laid the post across the wire, hoping that it contained no electrical warning device, pressed it down, and edged himself foot by foot across. The barbs reached up for his hands as though they were living creatures; he felt his trouser leg rip open, but at last he was over. The path wound on down through the garden, with a glimpse of the river through the trees, and ended at a wicket gate. He stepped through it on to the beach.

It had taken him three minutes to get so far and the cliff towered a sheer sixty feet above him. It looked loose and crumbling in the gloom and to his right he could see the entrance to one of the caves, packed tight with rubble to contain the explosion. For a second he thought of looking for the wire that led to the detonator, but gave up the idea at once. There were three separate charges and he would never find all of them in time. He took off his coat and started to drag himself up.

He had been right in thinking that the cliff would be loose. Lumps of soft sandstone and shale pulled away at a touch and fell in cascades to the beach. Ledges of grass that looked firm vanished under his weight and left him spread-eagled over nothing, but somehow he held on. Bit by bit, using his knees more than his feet, he dragged himself upwards. A shallow chimney filled with bracken gave him some protection, a short, jagged arete led to a wall of crumbling rock which seemed about to tilt forward on top of him, but at last he pulled himself over the edge.

There was still time. A little under half an hour to go and nobody could see him. A line of shrubs screened him from the floodlights and the hotel was barely fifty yards away, enormous and threatening with its towers and battlements looming up over the cliff and every window a blaze of light. Down the path he could see eyes coming towards him. A rabbit, two rabbits, three—a hare, a squirrel, a party of field mice, all rushing wildly past him as though he didn't exist. By some strange sense they must have known what was about to happen and were making for safety.

In the distance the community singing was still in progress. Against the wind which was starting to blow in from the sea, the tune of "Oh God Our Help in Ages Past" beat in time to his running feet. As he reached the hotel he saw that there was no way in through the main entrance. That was in full view of the crowd, but just to the right was a side door, open and swinging in the wind. He pushed through it and stepped inside.

He was in a huge, white-tiled kitchen, and as he looked around he realized just how urgent it must have been for Star Construction to get the cliff down before the approach of the cold spell. They hadn't even bothered to strip the place of its fittings. The cookers and basins and deep-freeze units had been removed, but the tiles themselves would have been worth a bit of money and a long run of copper pipe was still fixed to the wall. Star's contract must contain a heavy penalty clause for delays.

There was a baize door at the end of the kitchen. He passed through it, along a short passage, through another door and out into the main hall. In the glare of the naked lamps that had replaced the chandeliers, it looked like a film set of a cathedral, with fluted buttresses against the walls and tall pillars supporting the ceiling.

Yes, the old Royal really had been something all right. The inlaid marble floor which was big enough to have played football on led up to a reception desk the size of a fairly important post office and everywhere arrows pointed to its further amenities. The Lady Grey Restaurant—The Billiard Room—The South Riding Grill—The Felcliff Bar—The North Sea Cocktail Lounge—Library—Reading Room—Palm Court Ballroom. The whole place could have been still in use and for a moment he thought of taking a lift up to the third floor. At least those had been taken away, and there were blackened holes in the floor and ceiling to show where once the gilded cages had stood. On the wall beside them somebody had scratched "Sic transit gloria mundi" on the plaster.

Bill ran up the huge curving staircase. The carpets and banisters had been removed and his feet clicked like hammers on the marble steps. Though his one thought was to find those papers and get out before the explosion, images of balls and toastmasters and ladies in evening dress raced through his head.

First floor. Twenty-three minutes to go. Rooms 1–150, and long lines of doors running away down the corridors. Barber's Shop—Ladies' Hairdressing Salon—Ladies' and Gentlemen's Turkish Baths. Yes, quite a place, t'old Royal.

Second floor. Rooms 151–250. A discarded vacuum cleaner with no handle, a stuffed stag's head leering up at him from the landing, a broken chamber pot, a cracked mirror, an overturned fire bucket slopping sand. He hurried on up the next flight of stairs.

Third floor. A pile of torn blankets, a litter of newspapers, a heap of broken glass and plaster. Rooms 251–350 and an arrow pointing up to Roof Garden and Tennis Courts. The sound of the helicopter came in through an open window and the wind blew on his face. The cold, damp, sad wind of a midnight which was less than twenty minutes away.

Rooms 251–270–300–301. The door was open, swinging on its hinges and he stepped past it. The room in which Jumbo Wayne had stayed before his bungalow was ready for him: where he had sat and considered how much he and Mary could get for those papers. He could almost feel his presence there, though all the furniture had been removed, of course. Unfaded wallpaper showed where a wardrobe and a dressing table had stood and the French windows leading out to the balcony were open, swinging and grating together in the wind. Through them he could hear that the community singing was still in progress. Apparently the crowd had had their fill of religion and "Oh God Our Help in Ages Past" had been replaced by a raucous local ballad with an accordion leading the voices. "Oh, my girl's a Yorkshire girl, as everybody knows—Tararar —Tarar-ahm—"

A cupboard with the drawers pulled out, a telephone lying on the floor, a leaking radiator . . . "And though she's a factory lass and wears no fancy clothes . . ." The door to the bathroom . . . "I've a sort of Yorkshire relish for my little Yorkshire rose . . ."

"And what better place could Wayne have used to hide those papers?" Pode had said. "He knew that he would be the last occupant of the room and that it was not intended to strip the fittings before the demolition. As a senior executive of Star Construction he would have access there right up to the end.

"We should look for somewhere obvious, I think. Somewhere which your wife would have thought of straight away. An inspection trap to the pipes under the bath perhaps. If Wayne was a reader of spy stories, the lid of the lavatory cistern might have suggested itself to him."

Yes, Jumbo probably read a great many spy stories during his journeys up and down the country. Bill looked around the little green room. No inspection trap by the bath, but a low-level toilet suite. He lifted the lid and stared inside, seeing pipes, a black plastic ball and water turning brown with rust. No papers though, no package, but on the inside of the lid there were four white marks which might have been made by strips of sticky paper or tape. As he saw them he remembered the one vital thing he had forgotten. Just before Wayne knocked over the lamp he had told him what the letter said. The killer behind the curtains must have heard it too. In the bedroom a floorboard creaked and steps came towards him.

"Are you looking for something, Mr. Irwin? This perhaps?" Hans Witzleb smiled pleasantly at him and his stained teeth were like a line of brown pebbles in his little prim mouth. He held an envelope in his left hand and there was an automatic pistol in his right.

15

"Stand quite still please, Mr. Irwin, and I will give you an easy death. If you are stupid enough to move or try to rush me, it may be rather painful, I'm afraid." The smile had left Witzleb's face now and he looked completely bored and indifferent; a craftsman carrying out a dull and familiar piece of work which he had done a hundred times before. Bill watched the gun come up, saw his finger start to curl around the trigger and, though he was going to die, he felt nothing except contempt for himself. Nothing against Witzleb, nothing against Star who paid him, nothing except disgust at his own foolishness for forgetting that Wayne's killer must have heard him repeat the letter.

"No, Hans, not in the bathroom." Norman Star stood by the doors that led to the balcony, but he didn't look as though he had been hiding there. Like the German he looked bored and self-possessed. There was a cigar in his right hand and its inch of ash demonstrated the steadiness of his nerves.

"Would you step back in here, please, Mr. Irwin? Thank you." He motioned Bill into the bedroom and grinned at Witzleb.

"You always were a *dummer Kerl,* Hans. The bullet from that forty-five of yours could easily pass straight through his body and ricochet back to you off the tiles. That's right, Mr. Irwin, stand against the wall. Very well, Hans."

"But why? Sir Norman, you've got to tell me why?" Bill's words came gasping out and he could feel a tic beating in his forehead. He was going to die, but he had to know the whole story.

"Why are we going to kill you?" Star still sounded polite and indifferent. "Surely that's simple enough. Like your wife you discovered certain things about me and I can't afford to let you live."

"No, no, I don't mean that. I know why you've got to kill me now, but why the others? Mary, the lorry driver, Wayne? You murdered three people just because of that." He pointed at the envelope in Witzleb's left hand.

"We have no time for explanations." Witzleb stepped forward and the gun came up again. "I told them to blow on schedule whatever happens."

"And so they will, Hans, but we still have fifteen minutes to go and the question interests me." Star glanced at his watch. "Don't you think that those papers are a good enough reason for murder, Mr. Irwin? After all, they contain evidence which would almost certainly hang me."

"Hang you! Merely because they show that you got the Felcliff contract by bribery?"

"What? What do you say?" For a second there was a look of complete astonishment in Star's face and the ash fell from his cigar. "You still think that, do you? Mr. Irwin, you disappoint me. After all that has happened, you still believe the theory of that old fool Pode who has been on the wrong track from the beginning?

"No, Mr. Irwin, though I don't deny that certain people on the Council were persuaded to help me get the contract, those papers have nothing to do with it. You are a rather untrusting young man, I'm afraid. As I told you in London, they merely relate to a new type of cement."

"To cement! Then why? Why are they important? What makes you say that they could hang you?" Bill shook his head in bewilderment, but something was stirring in his memory. Pictures of grey figures cringing behind the wire of a concentration camp. The life story of a man with a scarred face and a burnt body in Hamburg that hadn't got a face at all. The public outcry when a Jewish businessman had offered a job to an ex-Nazi. The affectionate use of a German term *dummer Kerl*—"stupid fellow."

"It's clear enough, Mr. Irwin, if you'll only think a little. I say a new type of cement, but it isn't entirely new." Star dragged lightly on his cigar. "The process was actually perfected in a laboratory at Essen during the winter of '44, but all the data was destroyed during an R.A.F. bombing raid. When Hans came to England we started work on it again. We almost succeeded too, but your very intelligent wife found some of our notes, read through them and began to guess what they really meant. She then stole them and tried to blackmail me." He bowed slightly as though complimenting Mary's intelligence.

"Yes, your wife was a very bright girl, Mr. Irwin. You should be extremely proud of her. It was clever of her to see the significance of our notes, to remember that Organization K had been working on a similar project, to put two and two together so quickly. I am sincerely sorry that Hans killed her, but it was necessary to protect my own skin, as you say. Though it is almost twenty years ago, I still think that they would hang me.

"But surely you can guess the rest of it now. You see, my name is not really Star or Morgenstern, it is . . ."

"Your name is Willi Frenzel." Bill stared at the scarred, smiling face and in spite of everything he felt a sudden flicker of admiration. This was the one who got away—the one who fooled them all. Those scars had not been made by any whip in a concentration camp but by hurried plastic surgery before the Allied armies completely overran Germany.

"But I still don't understand. They found your body in the ruins of Hamburg."

"They found a body, Mr. Irwin. It was dressed in one of my uniforms, my identity tag was around its neck, but the face had been burned away by jellied phosphorus and it had nothing to do with me." He pulled a watch out of his pocket and glanced at it. "You will forgive me if I am brief. We have very few minutes left.

"I am a real German, Mr. Irwin, a Hitler German, but I have never been a dreamer. By the end of '44 I knew that the war was lost and I started to take precautions for the future. A double was found to impersonate me—the man whose body was discovered in Hamburg—and I entered a private hospital where things were done to alter my appearance. The S.S. supplied me with the dossier of one Emmanuel Morgenstern who had been destroyed at Buchenwald, and after a period of enforced starvation Obersturmbannführer Frenzel died and Morgenstern arrived at Rhuleben Concentration Camp. I have always been an excellent linguist, and my recently acquired Yiddish and Polish were good enough to satisfy everybody. The rest you know. I came to England and built this business. Three years ago I asked my old friend here to join me." He smiled at Witzleb with quite genuine affection. "Everything went all right, till one day your clever little wife walked into Herr Witzleb's office when he was out, saw those papers and guessed who I was. The price of her silence was to be a million pounds."

"It is time now, Willi. Stand away, please." Witzleb waved him to one side and raised the gun. Once again Bill saw his eyes glint behind the thick glasses.

"But you won't get away with it." Bill knew there was no hope for him, but he would at least play for time. "Pode knows about you. Besides, you'll never get through the barriers."

"Pode knows nothing, Mr. Irwin. By your own admission all he thinks about is some trumpery bribery charge which he can never prove. All the evidence will show that you were responsible for Wayne's death and fled the country." Star—Bill still couldn't think of his name as Frenzel—dropped the stub of his cigar and ground it out with his shoe.

"There is also no difficulty in our getting out of here. As soon as the lights are turned off we will simply walk to the barrier. The man who let us in will be off duty and nobody knows we are here. When we get to the gate they will open it for us. What could be more natural than the head of the firm and his chief engineer taking a final look around?

"I am personally very sorry to kill you, Mr. Irwin, but it is necessary, and I can promise you a fine tomb. Before the

month is finished your body will be under five feet of concrete." He turned away and nodded to Witzleb. "It is time to
go now, Hans. Ready?"

"*Fertig,* Willi." Witzleb raised the gun again, and though he
still looked bored and indifferent Bill sensed the satisfaction
that he must be feeling. Just one more murder and he and Star
would be safe and the past wiped out for ever.

But as he watched him, Bill suddenly knew that he had
one card left to play. Witzleb had an Achilles heel, and he had
shown it to him as they looked out through his office window
yesterday: a dislike of rats that had grown into mania. It was
a very small card, almost the lowest in the pack, but he had
nothing else. He forced his eyes away from the gun and stared
through the doorway.

"Look at them," he said. "Look at them behind you." He
heard his own voice rising to a scream. "The rats, Herr Witzleb! Dozens of them!"

Then he had him. For perhaps a second an expression of
loathing came into Witzleb's face, for a second he turned his
head and Bill was across the room and had grasped the barrel
of the gun. It swayed backwards and forwards between them,
swung against Bill's chest, slid past it and exploded. The blast
was like red hot metal against his flesh, but behind his back
he heard Star scream and Witzleb was reeling away with the
glasses dropping from his eyes and his breath roaring like a
broken-winded horse's on a hill. He hit Witzleb. He hit him in
the stomach with his fist. He hit him in the face with his fingers
outstretched and the nails slashing into his eyes. He hit him
with the flat of his hand, feeling the Adam's apple crush under
it and seeing the pistol fall as Witzleb staggered backward.
Back to the French window, back across the balcony, back to
the parapet; his hands clawing at it and his screams cut off by
the rattle of the helicopter overhead. For one long moment he
balanced there and then tilted head first into the night.

Bill looked down at the side of his chest. There was a blackened hole in his shirt and through it the flesh showed, red and

furrowed by the blast. The fight had seemed endless, but his watch was still working and the time was eight minutes to midnight. Ample time to reach safety. He kicked the pistol to one side and walked back into the bedroom. The envelope lay almost in the centre of the floor. He bent down and slipped it into his hip pocket.

"*Bitte—bitte schön,* Herr Irwin." Frenzel or Star stood, or rather hung, against the wall, and he looked as though he had been crucified. His arms were stretched out at shoulder level, the right hand gripping the frame of the door and the left a lamp bracket.

"Please—please, Mr. Irwin—help me." He swayed slightly and then fell as a tree falls; slowly at first, his fingers loosening from the door frame and leaving all his weight suspended from the lamp. For almost ten seconds he hung like that and then the bracket tore away from the wall and he crashed forward on to the floor. He lay there staring up at Bill and his right leg was bent out sideways like a broken hinge. Witzleb's bullet had shattered the kneecap.

"Mr. Irwin, help me please. In only a few minutes they will . . ."

"Yes, Sir Norman, or Herr Frenzel, whichever you prefer. In exactly seven minutes they will blow you to pieces." Bill looked down at him. Blood was dripping through the man's trouser leg and thickening in the dust on the floor. "But don't worry. You will have that fine concrete tomb you promised me. I wish you joy with it."

"No, no, don't leave me. I can pay you, Mr. Irwin. I can pay you so well, if you will take me with you. Please, please help me. A million pounds—what your wife asked for." His voice broke off into a sob. "For the love of God, Mr. Irwin."

For the love of God! There was something obscene in the plea—something petty. The man had killed his wife—had framed him for Wayne's death—had tried to enslave the world, but until he said that Bill had almost admired him.

"No," he said. "No, I'm damned if I'll help you, Herr Obersturmbannführer!" He walked out of the door and down the corridor.

Room 300–290–275–251, his feet clicked on the bare boards of the landing, the wind blew in through the open window, the sign pointed up to the roof garden, the pile of rubbish still lay at the top of the staircase. He slowed, paused, turned and walked back.

Star was through the doorway now. He was trying to pull himself down the corridor, half on his back, half on his side, and his leg was stretched out at an unnatural angle. He looked up and tried to smile as Bill came back to him. There were tears in his eyes and he had left a thick trail of blood behind him.

"So, so you came back, Mr. Irwin. You are a good man. I knew you would come back. A million pounds I can give you. Now, help me, please. Carry me out and don't let them . . ."

"No, I won't let them blow you up." Bill knelt down beside him. "Put your arms round my shoulders and hang on." He felt him do so and tried to pull himself to his feet, but it was no good. The huge body was like a lead weight—a tree rooted in the earth.

"No," he said. "No, we'll never make it that way. Let go of me and I'll run down and get them to stop the explosion."

"No, no, don't leave me, Mr. Irwin." Star's hands tightened. "I don't mind dying as long as you stay with me, but I can't die alone. No, I daren't die alone."

"But you bloody fool, there's no need for either of us to die—not yet." Bill tore at the fingers that held him to the floor. As he did so, he could see the seconds hand of his watch racing on towards the hour. "Your only chance is to let me go."

"My only chance?" Star nodded, but his fingers still held. "Yes, yes, perhaps you are right. And you promise, Mr. Irwin. You promise that you'll make them stop it?"

"Yes, I promise." The fingers went slack and Bill dragged himself to his feet. He turned and ran down the corridor to the stairs, and as he reached them he heard Star screaming behind him: "You promised, Mr. Irwin. Remember that you promised. Tell them that they can hang me if they like, but please—please don't let me die alone."

Six minutes to go. Only six minutes and it would be over. His feet slipped and slithered on the bare marble of the stairs and at each corner he almost fell into the well that the banisters had screened.

Second floor. The stag's head grinned at him as he passed and through the open window the red glow of the Star Construction sign mocked him. The sound of the helicopter was much fainter now. The pilot must have moved out to sea before the explosion.

The hall at last and still five and a half minutes to go. He ran through it, past the blackened lift shafts, the reception desk, the arrows pointing to the main entrance. The door was unlocked and he hurled it open, feeling wind and rain beat against his face. The instant that his feet reached the steps the lights went out.

"And here's a hand, my trusty friend—and gie's a hand o' thine." The crowd had burst into "Auld Lang Syne" in preparation for the end and everything was in darkness. The helicopter had switched off the lights on its fuselage and even the moon had slid behind a cloud, as though obeying Norman Star's instructions. Only the singing voices could help him find the barrier, and with the wind blowing up into a gale he couldn't really tell from where they were coming. He ran blindly in what he thought was the right direction, his feet stumbling across gravel, flowerbeds, a lawn, till at last he fell forward against something that tore and clawed at him: the wire.

"We twa ha' played about the braes and pulled the gowans fine . . ." The voices were just in front of him, but there was no post to help him over the wire this time. He raised it as high as he could with his hands and began to pull himself underneath. The barbs bit into his back like steel whips but at last he was under it. As he dragged himself up, the lights came on again. A battery of floodlights beamed full on the hotel and the crowd a solid black wall behind them.

Just three more minutes. He glanced at his watch as he ran forward. Star had a watch as well. He could imagine him staring at it before the hotel lights went out, listening to its tick in the darkness, seeing the seconds hand run forward in the glow of the floodlights. He could almost hear him screaming.

But he was over the rope and into the crowd. Smiling, singing faces were turning to looks of astonishment as he forced his way through them. A woman cried out, a child fell, somebody cursed and a hand clutched his shoulder, but he was through them and running towards the group by the tripod. There was a black box fixed on top of it now and the man he had seen at King's Cross was standing beside it.

"Superintendent, listen to me," he shouted. "Stop it—you must stop it. There's a man in there. For the love of God, Superintendent." Somehow Star's plea came automatically to his lips but it was almost drowned by the voice of the crowd. "We'll tak' a cup o' kindness yet, for the sake of auld lang syne."

"Superintendent, please listen to me."

"Oh no, not you again." The policeman swung round scowling. In the glare of the carbon lamps his eyes were an oddly bright green. "What's that you say? A man in there? What man?"

"It's Star—Sir Norman Star. No, no, that's not true." Somehow he couldn't find the right words. "His real name is Frenzel—Willi Frenzel."

"I see. Willi Frenzel, eh? That would be the ghost of the Nazi leader who was killed in '45, I suppose." The green eyes studied Bill's face and their expression altered. "No don't you worry any more about Frenzel, sir. He's very, very happy up there. Jackson!" He turned to a constable at his side. "You and Wallace take this gentleman along to the ambulance and go easy with him." He lowered his voice and tapped his forehead. "He's not just drunk, as I thought, but cracked; mad as a hatter."

"No, no, no, you must believe me." Bill tried to struggle but there was hardly any strength left in his body. Already the superintendent had moved away and was speaking to the man by the tripod. The black box had a T-shaped handle on top of it.

"All right, Mr. Denton," he said. "For God's sake let's get it over with before more of them go crazy." The crowd were quite silent now and Bill could hear him clearly as they dragged him back to the barrier. "Never mind about the exact timing. Blow her."

"In a minute, Superintendent. In just one minute. Sir Norman will have my hide if I don't keep to schedule. A real stickler for arrangements, Sir Norman is." Denton pulled out a watch and laid his hand on the plunger.

"Right. Thirty seconds—twenty—fifteen—ten—five— here we go." His face tensed and the handle went down.

There was hardly any noise at first. Just a low distant mutter and the ground moved very slightly. Then the sky sign Star Construction buckled, twisted, and went out. Below it the roof of the hotel vanished, the towers appeared to melt and a gable above the entrance split open. The mutter grew to a deep roar, the walls cracked and fell forward and there was suddenly no building there at all, but a huge dust cloud drifting up into the sky. Far below the cliff face bulged, reared up and curled; a vast avalanche of earth and rubble pouring down to the sea.

Bill closed his eyes. There was nothing more to do except close them and lean back against the strangely gentle arms that held him. As he did so he suddenly seemed to see Mary's face. It was a long way away, far too far away to really distinguish the features, but he knew that she was smiling at him.

www.ingramcontent.com/pod-product-compliance
Lightning Source LLC
Chambersburg PA
CBHW022011050726
47499CB00007BA/2232